We hope you enjoy this book.
Please return or renew it by the due date.
You can renew it at **www.norfolk.gov.uk/libraries**
or by using our free library app. Otherwise you can
phone **0344 800 8020** - please have your library
card and pin ready.
You can sign up for email reminders too.

CH

NORFOLK COUNTY COUNCIL
LIBRARY AND INFORMATION SERVICE

D0231263

A MESSAGE FROM CHICKEN HOUSE

This is Dan's greatest novel. There, I've said it. I've been thrilled and excited by his stories before – but never this moved by mystery and family feeling. This is a story about coming home to a strange land with an even stranger inheritance – to forge a bond where you appear to be unwanted and to reach beyond the grave to find love and belonging. It's thrilling and dangerous and unexpected too!

BARRY CUNNINGHAM
Publisher
Chicken House

NISHA'S WAR

DAN SMITH

2 PALMER STREET, FROME, SOMERSET BA11 1DS

WWW.CHICKENHOUSEBOOKS.COM

Text © Dan Smith 2022
Illustration © Matthew Land 2022

First published in Great Britain in 2022
Chicken House
2 Palmer Street
Frome, Somerset BA11 1DS
United Kingdom
www.chickenhousebooks.com

Chicken House/Scholastic Ireland, 89E Lagan Road, Dublin Industrial Estate,
Glasnevin, Dublin D11 HP5F, Republic of Ireland

Cover and interior design by Steve Wells
Typeset by Dorchester Typesetting Group Ltd
Printed and bound in Great Britain by CPI Group (UK) Ltd, Croydon, CR0 4YY

FSC
www.fsc.org
MIX
Paper from
responsible sources
FSC® C020471

13 5 7 9 10 8 6 4 2

British Library Cataloguing in Publication data available.

ISBN 978-1-912626-75-5
eISBN 978-1-913696-16-0

For Dad. We miss you.

Barrow Island
haunts me.

I think it always
will. No matter where
I go, whatever I do,
a part of me will
always stay behind
on Barrow Island.

MARCH 1942

NINE DAYS UNTIL FULL MOON

REFUGEES

The train crawled into Bealmouth and groaned to a halt. There was no clatter of doors as passengers disembarked from dark and lonely carriages. There was no quiet bustle of relatives meeting, or of young soldiers uttering last farewells.

Here, on a grey spring evening, only one door opened at that desolate station. Only two wretched figures stepped down on to the platform. A broken-hearted woman and her thirteen-year-old daughter. Ragged and exhausted, they were hardly more than skin and bone. Travellers from another time and place.

They stood in the steam like ghosts in the fog.

Both Mother and Daughter flinched when the guard's whistle screamed loud and shrill. They huddled together as the train huffed and puffed, and dragged itself away into the cold.

And then there was only the wind.

They had nothing with them but the clothes they wore. Mother's colourful sari was long gone. Daughter's favourite dress was a distant memory. Instead, Mother wore thick woollen trousers given to her on the ship, and a stout pair of men's shoes that gaped around her thin ankles. Daughter wore pink pyjamas donated by a kind lady with sad eyes at Glasgow station. A threadbare coat hardly kept the wind from chilling her bones, and a pair of someone else's shoes pinched her bare toes.

As she looked along the empty platform, Daughter put a hand in her pocket and closed her fist around the small red stone she had carried from the other side of the world. It was her little piece of home. Whenever she looked at it, she was reminded of sunshine and colour and sweetness.

Now, though, everything was grey.

The platform was grey. The small stone station house was grey. The sky was grey. Even the air was grey.

And although it was March, she could see her warm breath in the cold air. Like steam from a train.

'They should be expecting us,' Mother said into the silence.

She was a shadow of what she had been just ten weeks ago. Life on board the ship had been cruel, and now Mother's skin was stretched tight around her cheekbones. Her eyes were sunken and bloodshot. Her black hair had lost its shine. But what bothered Daughter most of all was that Mother hadn't stopped shivering since they boarded the train at Glasgow.

'Come along.' Mother smiled as best as she could.

Without another word, the two refugees made their way along the platform towards the station exit.

Outside, a narrow lane stretched in both directions. It was lined with tall hedges and lonely trees. There was no sign of life except for the hungry sparrows flitting among the leafless branches.

'Perhaps we could walk.' Mother looked both ways along the lane. 'Which way do you think it is?'

Before Daughter could reply, a dusky blur of crows rose above the trees in the distance. They scattered into the air caw-cawing and circling like dark spirits in the grey sky. When they settled, there came a strange and gentle clip-clopping sound.

The clip-clopping persisted, growing louder, as if the Devil himself were dancing in the mist.

Mother and Daughter waited with unease until finally a dark brown pony appeared around the corner of the lane, pulling a small trap. The trap wasn't anything special – just a rickety seat attached to a pair of large wheels. A man sat upon it, wrapped in a heavy overcoat. A flat cap was pulled low over his brow.

'Do you think he's here for us?' Mother whispered.

2

HOME

Mother and Daughter waited by the side of the road as the pony and trap slowed to a halt. The driver was old with a weathered face. His skin was rough bark on an ancient tree, and he hunched his shoulders beneath his thick coat as if he were not quite human. Everything about him looked as if it belonged to the land. He steadied the pony and slowly lifted his head to watch Mother and Daughter with watery blue eyes. They were the most colourful thing in that cold and grey place.

'Mrs Barrow?' His voice was deep and soft.

'Yes,' Mother replied.

'I'm Mr Foster. Mrs Barrow sent us to fetch you. The

other Mrs Barrow, I mean.' His accent was strange, and his words tumbled over each other.

'Thank you.' Mother approached the trap, still holding Daughter's hand.

'Any luggage?' The trap creaked as the man rose. 'I'll help you—'

'We don't have anything,' Mother said. 'It's just us.'

'Right you are then.' He eased himself back into the seat and stared straight ahead.

Mother paused, looked the trap once over, then climbed aboard and shuffled up next to the driver. Daughter followed, pulling the threadbare coat tight over her knees for warmth.

As soon as they were settled, the driver snapped the reins and the pony clip-clopped along the lane until they came to a place wide enough to turn around and head back.

'Has there been any word from my husband?' Mother asked. 'Mr Barrow, that is?'

'There's been nowt yet.' The driver kept his eyes ahead as he spoke. 'You're lucky we got word from you. Not much is getting through these days. There's a war on you know.'

Mother shivered and lowered her head. 'Is it far to the island?'

'It'll not be long.' The man blinked away the water in his eyes.

'Thank you.' Mother looked up at him. 'My daughter's name is Nisha. And I'm—'

'Mrs Barrow,' the man said. 'I know.'

The pony took them along the lane between the hedges, and out among endless fields where every inch of soil was turned and furrowed. Isolated farmhouses stood defiant on desolate hilltops or lay hidden in sunken valleys.

The trap rattled on and on until houses came into view, and the air grew colder. Here, there was a thick, salty smell of the sea that made Nisha's stomach tighten with fear.

Mr Foster was saying something Nisha couldn't hear, so she leant forward and tilted her head. But even then, his accent was difficult to understand, and some of his words were unfamiliar.

'. . . not much here but it's enough. We call it Morbury,' he said as the pony took them past the first houses and into the village. 'Mind, you'll not find any signs, because they come and took 'em all down. Divvent want the Germans to knaa where they're gannin' if they ever get ashore.'

Mostly it was a disorderly muddle of stone cottages with grey slate roofs, and small front gardens. An old man working on his vegetable patch stopped and leant on his spade as he watched them. A small, wiry-haired terrier scrambled to the gate and growled. A couple of children playing on the path stopped, too, as if they'd never seen such a thing as three people riding a pony and trap.

In the heart of the village there was a handful of shops. A few people were going about their business but when the trap passed by, everybody stopped. A small group of women nudged each other and turned to see the refugees. Children ceased playing. Even the shopkeepers, still in their aprons, came out to watch.

Nisha turned to look over her shoulder, but everyone was still just standing there, staring.

'It's fine, darling,' Amma whispered to her. 'Take no notice. We're going to be all right now. We're safe. I promise.'

Leaving the village behind, Mr Foster steered the trap through the complicated concrete roadblock and followed a narrow track between the fields until they finally emerged on to the coast.

In the distance a mist hung over the churning, grey North Sea. And there, breaking out from the wet sand, Nisha's new home loomed like a monster in the mist.

Barrow Island.

3

A LONELY SHADOW

Barrow Island was grey and rocky and unwelcoming. Hunched in the surf beyond the long, flat stretch of wet sand, it didn't belong to the world. At first it was impossible to see anything but its shape through the fret, but as they drove on to the causeway, more of the island came into view. Soon Nisha saw the beach and the road leading up to the house that stood exactly dead centre of the island.

At the northernmost tip, above the cliffs, stood the silhouette of what appeared to be a small castle.

'Where we are right now,' Mr Foster said, 'will be sea before you knaa it.'

The wind muffled Mr Foster's words so that Nisha caught only the sense of what he'd said, but it was enough to make her stiffen. She shifted closer to Amma and closed her eyes.

Amma gave her hand a reassuring squeeze.

'Soon as the tide comes in, it'll cut us off,' Mr Foster went on. 'This causeway is the only way on and off the island, and only when nature allows it. But we're all right for now.'

Nisha summoned the courage to open her eyes and look out.

The causeway was a narrow stone path that curved across the mud and sand towards Barrow Island. It was strewn with tentacles of seaweed as if to remind travellers that the choking sea would soon return to claim it. A carpet of a thousand-thousand shells popped and crunched beneath the trap's wheels. Worm-cast twists of wet mud and corpses of old driftwood littered the sand at either side. Miniature mountain ranges of slippery rocks trapped struggling crabs in rippling rock pools. But in contrast to the natural order, a line of mysterious concrete blocks stretched like strange invaders in both directions.

'Ironside's Crust,' Mr Foster said. 'There's them what think the Germans are gonna invade from over there.' He pointed beyond the island. 'And them blocks are supposed to stop tanks, but they'll have to be quicker than a dog on a hare if they want to bring tanks in 'ere. Soon as the tide starts comin' in, she comes in fast. Them blocks'll be twenty feet under the waves before the hour's done, and you'd best remember *that* should you ever want to be off the island.'

Nisha gripped Amma's hand and looked back towards the shore. Towards the safety of the land they had left behind.

'She's sneaky,' Mr Foster said. 'Like a fox. She'll sweep in behind you as well as comin' in from the front, and if that happens, the only hope you've got is that refuge hut.' He pointed to a small hut on stilts that stood halfway along the causeway. Rickety wooden steps led up to an open doorway. 'You get trapped by the tide, that's where you gan else get washed out to sea. But the best thing is to be sure it doesn't happen at all.' He leant across to look at her. 'You hear?'

Nisha nodded and stared into his watery eyes. When he went back to watching the causeway, though, she turned her face towards the island and let the damp air needle her skin.

They followed the causeway as it curved south then snaked its way up on to the island and through the grassy dunes towards the house. Nisha felt a flutter of relief once they were on dry land and the sea was safely behind them.

As they crested the rise, Nisha had her first proper look at Barrow House.

The large grey building was as different from her true home as it could be. It was big enough for ten families to live in, with three sets of enormous chimneys, and an imposing covered entrance. On the second floor, above the main doorway, was a balcony with grey stone spindles blackened by time and weather. The dark grey slate roof was spotted with dull patches of moss, and there were places where tiles had slipped free and had not been replaced. Stone walls were pitted and blackened. The white paint around the window frames was faded and cracked.

Above it, the ghost of a crescent moon winked from behind the veil of cloud and mist.

Trundling up towards the house, Nisha looked across to the castle and saw that it was a crumbling ruin. Only the half-collapsed shell of one tower remained. It stood on the clifftop like a decayed and broken tooth. Close to it, a distorted, leafless tree was silhouetted against the sky. It rose from the island as an ugly claw of twisted branches stretching upwards and outwards. And in its knotted fingers it grasped a dilapidated tree house.

In the darkness beneath the tree house stood a lonely shadow blacker than despair. Indistinct, it was neither one thing nor another. Just a wretched emptiness in the evening. The sight of it made Nisha's bones ache with cold. She wanted to look away, but couldn't. Drawn to the strangeness of it, she wiped her eyes and squinted through the drizzle, trying to make out what it was. As the pony and trap took them onwards, wheels clattering on the track, the blackness began to take shape. It was as if the darkness were changing; becoming. Nisha could see now that the shadow was, in fact, a person.

No. Not just a person.

A child.

There was a boy standing beneath the tree. Dark and alone and unafraid.

Somehow, Nisha knew he was following their progress towards the house. She felt his watchful gaze fall over them. She felt his sadness.

Just then, the icy wind picked up and Nisha heard someone whisper her name.

'Hm?' She turned to Amma.

'Nothing, darling,' Amma said. 'I didn't say anything.'

Nisha frowned and looked back at the boy standing beneath the tree.

But he was gone.

4
A COLD RECEPTION

By the time they reached Barrow House, the sky was almost dark. Mr Foster brought the pony to a halt by the entrance, and the three of them sat listening to the quiet music of rain pattering on the ground. Beyond it was the bluster of the wind, and embracing it all was the steady crash of the cruel sea against the crag at the north end of the island.

'Is there anyone home?' Amma asked as she shifted along the seat. She indicated that Nisha should get down from the trap. 'I don't see any lights.'

'It's dangerous to let the lights show,' Mr Foster said. 'Mrs Foster will be out any minute to take you inside.

She'll look after you, Mrs Barrow.'

'Please. Call me Rani.'

'I'll stick with Mrs Barrow if it's all the same.'

Nisha jumped down on to the gravel that covered the circular driveway, then turned to help Amma.

When Nisha touched Amma's skin, it felt hotter than it ought to. Her eyes were bloodshot and her lips were pale.

'I'll be fine,' she said when she noticed Nisha watching her.

They approached the house and stepped under the covered entrance. Amma reached for the bell but before she could ring it, the door swung open.

'Eee, let's get you two inside,' said the woman who stood in the shadows. She spoke with the same broad accent as Mr Foster. 'You look like drowned rats in a poor man's cellar. You must be half frozen, and soaked to the bone.'

She ushered them inside and closed the door.

The vast hallway was cold and unwelcoming. There was no light except for the day's last dregs filtering in through the high windows. Paintings hung on the wood-panelled walls, but it was too dark to see what they were. In the centre of the hallway, an enormous staircase headed straight up and split left and right to join a square gallery that ran around the entire floor above. It would have been easy to believe that ghosts hid in the darkness up there, looking down at the refugees.

'Fancy havin' to arrive on a day like this.' The woman fussed about them, taking their coats, while they stood dripping on the stone floor. 'Can't have you in these wet things, you'll catch your death. And we definitely divvent—'

Just then the door to Nisha's left opened and the glow of a fire slipped into the hallway. A small dog scuttled out and ran around Nisha's legs. She crouched to pet him. The dog wagged his tail, and pushed his nose into Nisha's hand, sniffing the red stone she had saved from her pocket before the woman took her coat.

'Humphrey! Heel!' A harsh voice bellowed from the study and the dog hurried back in, toenails clicking on the stone floor.

A moment later, a tall, thin woman appeared. She stood in the orange light, straightened her skirt with both hands, then strode into the hallway like a sergeant major. Back straight, chin high. She had steel hair flecked with iron filings, and her heels click-clacked on the stones as if she were important.

'I'm Mrs Barrow,' she said. The way she spoke was clear and perfect. Not at all like Mr and Mrs Foster.

'I'm Mrs— Rani. I'm Rani. It's a pleasure to meet you, Mrs Barrow. I just wish it was under better circumstances.' Amma stepped forward and held out her hand.

'Hm.' Mrs Barrow looked at Amma's hand as if it might be poisonous, then she took it with a limp grip, shook once, and let go.

Nisha noticed that Mrs Barrow wiped her hand on her skirt afterwards.

'And this is Nisha,' Amma said.

Nisha stepped forward and raised her hand towards her grandmother, but Mrs Barrow ignored her.

'Mrs Foster will get you settled,' she said. 'She'll give you something to eat, show you to your rooms, and find you some clothes.' She looked Nisha up and down with distaste.

Nisha suddenly felt very aware that she was standing in the cold hallway wearing only a pair of pink pyjamas.

'Mrs Foster will also tell you the rules,' said Mrs Barrow. 'Please make sure you obey them at all times.' She looked at Amma. 'Both of you.'

With that, she returned to the study and closed the door.

5

THE RULES

'You'll get used to 'er.' Mrs Foster lowered her voice
when Nisha's grandmother had locked herself away.
'She's a bit spiky and it seems like she's always in bad
fettle, but she's not so bad once you get to know her.'

'Fettle?' Amma asked.

Mrs Foster smiled. 'Mood. It seems like she's always
in a bad mood.'

Nisha and her mother followed the housekeeper along
a gloomy corridor panelled with too much dark wood.
At the far end, a narrow back-staircase climbed up into
the darkness. Mrs Foster led them to a door at the foot of
the staircase and pushed it open. It swung inwards with

a tired creak, revealing the world hidden behind it.

The square kitchen was huge and warm. It smelt like cooking and baking and laundry and soap all mixed up in one confused muddle. Almost every inch of wall space was lined with cupboards and shelves, some of them bearing so much weight that they bowed in the middle.

At the far end was a sink big enough to bathe in. Above it, a window looked out at the back of the house. A courtyard of stone buildings was just visible through the condensation that ran in tracks down the glass.

One side of the room was completely occupied by a range big enough for ten cooks at once. In front of it stood a large wooden table laden with weighing scales, and bowls, and jars and tins of all shapes and sizes. Hanging from hooks above it was a torrent of pots and pans, which looked as if they were hundreds of years old.

On another table, beside the stone sink, was a large wireless. It was switched on, but turned so low it was just a murmur of voices.

A black-and-white cat slept on the mat in front of the range.

'Sit yoursel' down,' Mrs Foster said. 'I'll hang these wet things up then get you summat to eat.' She lowered the drier that swung over the range and spread the coats out while Amma struggled to pull two chairs from under the table. Nisha stood and waited as she dragged them close to the range, then they sat down and huddled together.

'Better?' Amma pulled Nisha against her. 'Feeling warmer?'

Nisha answered by pressing herself tighter against her mother.

'Right.' Mrs Foster straightened her apron and busied around behind them, clattering cutlery and crockery. She took a huge fire-blackened pan from a hook over the table and placed it on the range. Soon, a delicious smell filled the room.

After a few minutes, Mrs Foster handed them each a plate. 'It's not much,' she said, 'but it's better 'n nowt.'

Nisha shifted the red stone into her left hand and took her plate without a word.

'Thank you, Mrs Foster,' Amma said. 'You're very kind.'

'Kindness has nowt to dee with it; it's common decency. Anyway, it's me job to look after you, and lookin' at the sorry state of you both, I'm thinkin' you must be starvin'. Oh, and you can stop with all that "Mrs Foster" carry-on. Call me Mrs F like everyone else.'

Amma forced a smile. 'Thank you, Mrs F.'

Nisha looked at the thin sandwich on her plate. The bread was browned from the frying pan.

'If you're wonderin' what's in there,' Mrs F said, 'it's Spam. The Americans have started sending it over, and it's not too bad if you fry it up with the bread. Anyway, there's nowt much else to be had these days, so we make do with what we've got.'

It looked nothing like Nisha was used to at home. There was no rich colour, no strong and spicy smell, but it definitely smelt better than anything she had eaten on the ship. And when she took a bite, she was surprised it tasted as good as it did. She hadn't eaten anything with flavour for weeks, but this was hot and greasy and delicious.

'You like that, eh?' Mrs F smiled. 'Aye, well, it makes a change from tripe. And I won't have that National Loaf rubbish – it's like Hitler's secret weapon – so I sieve me flour to make decent bread.'

Amma started to nibble the corner of her sandwich but was overcome by an attack of shivering. The sandwich tumbled from her hand, and the plate crashed to the floor, shattering into pieces.

The cat yowled and scooted away under the table.

Nisha stopped chewing. She put her plate on the table and grabbed Amma's hand. She squeezed tight, not wanting to let go.

'It's all right.' Amma's teeth chattered as she spoke. 'I'm fine.' She glanced up at Mrs F, but her eyes were moving from side to side as if she couldn't focus. 'I'm . . . sorry. About the plate.'

'Eee, you poor thing.' Mrs F picked up the broken pieces of crockery. 'Divvent fret about the plate, we've got enough plates to have the whole army round for tea. And I can keep your sandwich for later – I reckon now's a good time to get you into a hot bath. I set the copper boiling not long after Mr Foster went for you, so it should be ready.'

Mrs F put the pieces of broken plate on the table.

'I'll fetch the tub from the scullery.' She disappeared through a door in the corner of the kitchen and reappeared a few moments later carrying a large tin bath which she set on the mat in front of the range.

'Only supposed to have five inches.' Mrs F pointed at the white line hand-painted around the inside of the tub. 'But I think we can make an exception today, don't you?' She winked. 'Not a word to anyone, mind.'

She looked down at Nisha. 'Eat up and you can give us a hand. With two of us workin', we'll have it filled in no time.'

Nisha looked at Amma, who nodded once and tried to smile. 'Go on,' she managed. 'I'll be fine.'

Nisha finished her sandwich in a couple of bites. She sucked her fingers clean then followed Mrs F down into the scullery. Smaller than the kitchen, the room had its own sink and table. A washing line ran from one end to the other. Piles of laundry baskets were stacked against the wall.

The housekeeper passed Nisha a bucket and showed her how to draw water out of the large copper in the corner.

Mrs F was right; with two of them working, the tub

was filled in no time. As soon as it was ready, Nisha helped Amma undress and climb in. She sat shivering with her arms wrapped around herself.

Nisha knelt beside the tub and trailed her hands in the water.

'I've never had a hot bath before,' Amma said. 'It's good.'

'Do you not wash where you're from?' Mrs F pulled a face.

Nisha turned and tilted her head to listen.

'Of course,' Amma said. 'But not in a tub. And we don't heat the water.'

'Oh. Well. I suppose it would cool you off in all that sunshine. It must be nice to be warm all year round.'

Nisha closed her eyes and wished she was back home where the sun always shone. She longed to wear a soft cotton dress and run barefoot on the grass. She wanted to be out in the field with Papa, feeling his excitement as they watched a hornbill spread its wings across the forest.

'So,' said Mrs F. 'I'd best get to them rules Mrs Barrow mentioned.'

Nisha opened her eyes and was back in the kitchen. 'Pardon?'

'D'you know?' said Mrs F in surprise. 'That's the first word I've heard you speak since you got 'ere. D'you not talk?'

Nisha looked down.

'She talks.' Amma's voice was quiet, but at least she had stopped shivering quite so much. 'But not like she used to. Not since what happened. And she doesn't hear so well now.'

Nisha tightened her fingers around the stone. She tried not to think about the screaming and the crying that wouldn't go away.

'It's her right ear,' Amma said. 'It happened in Singapore. Nisha doesn't like to talk about it.'

'That's all right, pet.' Mrs F leant forward and patted Nisha's arm. When she was close like that, Nisha could see the grey roots of her coal-black hair.

'If you divvent want to talk, that's fine by me,' said Mrs F. 'I'll just tell you the rules, such as they are.' She took a deep breath. 'No lights unless absolutely necessary. There's blackout curtains over all the windows to stop leaks, but we divvent want mistakes so it's best not to have any lights at all if we divvent need 'em. Hitler uses the island as a landmark for flying north and south to bomb the shipyards, and you divvent want that on your conscience, do you?'

Nisha shook her head and tried not to think about David Hill and the awful thing that had happened. She would never be able to put it right.

'If the planes come, we're supposed to gan to the shelter out back.' Mrs F pointed towards the kitchen window. 'Except Mrs Barrow never obeys that rule. Whenever I tell her to come to the shelter, she just tells me nee foreigner is going to chase her out of her home.' As she said it, Mrs F caught Nisha's eye and flushed with embarrassment.

'Umm . . .' She looked away. 'Divvent play in the ruined Keep – that's the castle up on the crag – and divvent climb the Weepin' Tree. In fact, divvent gan near there at all. That's another rule.'

'The Weeping Tree?' Amma asked.

'Aye.' Mrs F's face darkened as if a thunderhead had passed across it. 'It's the tree on the crag, an' it's dangerous so stay away from it. An' if you cross to the mainland, make sure you know the tide 'cause you divvent want to get trapped on the causeway when the sea sweeps round. Too many people have drowned that way. And divvent get under Mrs Barrow's feet. She's a stickler for . . .'

But Nisha wasn't listening any more; she was thinking about the Weeping Tree, and the figure she had seen standing beneath it.

6

SPOOKY OLD HOUSE

By the time Mrs F showed them to their rooms, the day was gone and Barrow House was in darkness. Mrs F carried a lamp with a candle inside it, lighting the way up the creaking staircase. The cold surrounded them. It chilled Nisha despite the warm nightclothes and thick socks Mrs F had found for her. It undid all the good work of the hot meal and the cosy kitchen.

'I suppose you're used to having the lekky,' Mrs F said. 'Electric, I mean. But it hasn't come to Barrow Island yet, nor to most of the village, for that matter. There's no telephone, neither, an' if you want water it comes fresh from the pump. None of your mod cons here.'

At the top of the stairs, the landing ran around the hallway in a square. Mrs F took them to the right and along a passageway directly above the one which led to the kitchen.

'This'll be you, Mrs Barrow.' Mrs F opened the first door with a creak. 'And Nisha can go next door.'

Nisha nudged Amma and shook her head.

'We'll sleep in the same room,' Amma said to Mrs F. 'Thank you.'

Mrs F smiled and nodded. 'Keep the bairn close in this spooky old house, eh?' She winked at Nisha.

'Bairn?' Amma asked.

'Aye, the young 'un,' Mrs F said. 'The bairn.' She bent down to look at Nisha. 'I know it's a bit creepy here, but there's nowt to worry about, pet. There's nee one on the island but those you've already seen.'

'What about the boy?' Nisha asked.

'Boy?' Mrs F leant back and shook her head. 'There's no boy here. There's no one here but us.'

'But I saw him,' Nisha said. 'By the tree.'

'Must've been the shadows playin' tricks,' Mrs F said. 'This place'll do that sometimes. Barrow Island can make you think you saw summat that was never there.'

Before Nisha could say anything else, Mrs F fished some candles from the front pocket of her apron. She handed them to Amma, along with a box of matches. 'In case you need light,' she said. 'But be sure to keep the curtains closed. We divvent want anythin' leaking out and giving Hitler a place to bomb.'

'Thank you.' Amma fumbled the candles. They clattered to the floor and rolled in all different directions.

Without a word, Nisha got to her knees and collected them, feeling about in the shadows for any stragglers.

'Sure you're all right, pet?' Mrs F raised the lamp to look at Amma's face.

'I just need to sleep.' Amma wiped away the beads of sweat glistening on her brow.

'Aye, well,' Mrs F said. 'The bed's made up, and the curtains is drawn, and there's a commode for if you get caught short in the night. I've put clothes out for you for tomorrow, so I hope they fit. Goodnight and sleep well.' She turned and made her way back along the passageway, taking the light with her. As she reached the landing, she paused and turned to look over her shoulder at Nisha and Amma.

'Oh. And welcome to Barrow House.'

7
DARK SHAPES AND
STORMY SEAS

Springs sagged and creaked when Amma and Nisha climbed into the enormous bed. The sheets were like ice so Nisha huddled close to Amma. She closed her eyes and listened to the muffled crash and roar of the sea beyond the blackout curtain. When she had left the ship, she had wished never to be near the sea again. It took everything away. There was too much despair in its valleys and peaks. And yet here she was, cast adrift on a rocky ship in the grip of a cold cold sea.

Down and down into the dark. Nisha shook the thought away.

'Do you think Papa is all right?' she whispered.

'Of course.' Amma wrapped her arms around Nisha and squeezed tight.

Amma's skin was hot like she was burning.

'Not feeling any better?' Nisha asked.

'I'll be fine, my little *bairn*.' Amma giggled.

Nisha giggled too, but she stopped herself. 'It doesn't feel right when Papa might be in trouble. We don't even know where he is.'

'I believe he caught a ship just after us,' Amma said. 'He'll probably arrive in the next few days.'

'Promise?'

'I promise.'

'I don't think she likes us,' Nisha said.

'Mrs F? She seems kind.'

'No, my grandmother. She's . . .' But Nisha couldn't think of the right word.

'Stern?' Amma suggested.

'Cold,' Nisha said.

'Give her time,' Amma replied. 'To her we're different. She just needs to get used to us.'

'Different how?'

'We're not English.'

'I'm *half* English.'

'Yes, you are, my darling, but it's the other half she needs to get used to. The Indian half. And we'll get used to her too, I'm sure.'

They talked for a while longer, but Amma's voice grew faint and drowsy and soon her breathing settled into the regular rhythm of sleep.

Sleep didn't come so quickly to Nisha, though. It floated around her like a phantom, sometimes half taking her, but always letting go at the last moment. It was as if the island wanted to keep her somewhere between awake and asleep so it could hear her thoughts.

Into her exhaustion came guilt and fear and hopelessness. There were images of ships and bombs, and planes diving from the sky. There was the pale face of a boy called David. There was the overwhelming panic of the sea dragging her into its suffocating embrace.

Down and down into the dark.

Nisha woke with a jolt and found herself thinking about the Weeping Tree standing on the crag, and the figure she had seen beneath it.

And she heard her name in the wind.

She lifted her head from the pillow and looked towards the window. Something drew her there, so she climbed quietly from the warmth of the bed and crept over. Standing in the aching cold, Nisha opened the blackout curtain just enough to look out. Thick clouds smothered the moon and stars so that the darkness was never-ending. She saw nothing but tiny flecks of rain spattering the glass like mournful tears. She heard nothing but the wind and the sea battling the night.

As she stood, the raindrops became larger and more persistent. They rattled to come inside, tapping and drumming like unsettled spirits. Somewhere out at sea, the storm flickered bright white, just for an instant. A few seconds later, thunder broke in the distance. It announced itself with a sharp crack followed by a long rumble, as if the sky had torn in two.

Nisha put her face closer to the window, peering into the night. She waited for the lightning to come again.

When it did, night turned to day.

The whole world flared and flickered. It lasted only a second or two, but in that instant, she had a clear view of the beach at the south end. And when she looked towards the north end, she saw a large walled area not far from the house. Beyond that, the skeleton of the ruined Keep stood on the crag, with the Weeping Tree close by.

The tree rose from the ground like a gnarled hand reaching out from within the cruel island. The fingers were twisted branches that curled like claws, and below them was the same shadowy blackness she had seen earlier.

The shape of a child was standing beneath the tree.

A boy.

Alone in the storm.

He was facing the house, and although Nisha couldn't see anything more than his dark shape, she was sure he was looking right at her.

An icy fist tightened in her stomach. Her breathing quickened and she gripped the windowsill with both hands. Nisha wanted to turn and flee to the safety of bed, but something held her at the window, spellbound. Tears sprang into her eyes as she stared unblinking at the dark figure. It looked deep into her; crawling over her thoughts, searching her heart. Finding her weakness.

It felt like an eternity. The figure beneath the tree. Nisha at the window. The two of them locked together.

Then, finally, the shadow shifted. It didn't walk, or run, or jump. It slid sideways, to join the shape of the tree, and was gone.

Nisha trembled as thunder rolled out across the sea once more, shaking the island to its soul. Then night reclaimed the tree and the world fell back into darkness.

And the spell was lifted.

The island released her and, without a second thought, Nisha turned and ran back to bed. She jumped under the covers, squeezed herself tight against Amma, and pulled the thick blankets over her head. Huddled like that, she shivered and wondered about the dark figure beneath the Weeping Tree.

It was a long time before she fell asleep.

EIGHT DAYS UNTIL FULL MOON

8

FROM BAD TO WORSE

Nisha woke up with a start.

'Amma! What's wrong?'

Amma was curled into a ball at the far edge of the bed. She had thrown off the covers and was shivering uncontrollably. Her skin was burning up as if she were on fire, her nightdress was soaked with sweat, and when Nisha touched her, Amma pulled away as if it were painful. She stretched her legs out, then pulled them back towards her chest, mumbling words that made no sense.

'Amma, please. Stop.'

Amma's eyes opened just a fraction. 'Nisha . . . I'm . . .' she managed to say before her eyes rolled up in her head.

'Amma?'

Amma didn't respond. All she did was lie there shivering, and Nisha knew she had to get help.

Without wasting a moment, she leapt out of bed and ran to the door. She yanked it open and sprinted along the passageway and out on to the landing. She grabbed the bannister to help her turn the corner at speed, then raced down the stairs, taking them two at a time.

'I'll have no running in the house, thank you!' came a stern voice from the study.

Nisha ignored her grandmother and hurried along the downstairs passage, barging her shoulder against the last door and almost falling into the kitchen. There was no sign of Mrs F so Nisha ran into the scullery, where she found the housekeeper on her hands and knees, scrubbing the floor. When Nisha burst in, Mrs F jumped in surprise and flicked the brush across the stone tiles. 'Blimey, pet, you nearly gave us a heart attack.'

Nisha stood in front of her, trying to make her voice work.

'Heavens above.' Mrs F struggled to her feet. 'You look like you've seen a ghost.'

Nisha went to her, grabbed hold of Mrs F's apron and started pulling her towards the kitchen.

'What is it, pet? What on earth's the matter?'

'Come quickly,' Nisha gasped. 'Amma's dying.'

9

TICK-TOCK

Upstairs, Amma was lying in the same position as she had been when Nisha woke up. She was shivering violently.

Mrs F frowned and shook her head. 'I'm nee doctor, pet, but I'm sure she's not dying.'

There was a serious look on her face, though.

'Looks to me like some kind of flu,' said Mrs F. 'I'll send Mr Foster to fetch Doctor Michaels. He's a bit doddery, but he's a good man and mostly knows what he's deein'.'

It was a good hour and a half before Doctor Michaels

arrived. Nisha watched every minute pass by on the clock that stood on the stone mantelpiece over the fireplace.

Tick-tock.

Time inched past. Nisha only looked away to check on Amma.

Tick-tock.

Doctor Michaels was a small man with a large stomach that strained at the buttons of his jacket. He had a wrinkly neck like a turtle, and wore small round spectacles perched on the end of his long nose.

He gave Nisha a cursory nod when he came into the bedroom, and went straight to Amma. He checked her over, taking instruments and paraphernalia from the well-used Gladstone bag that he left open on the floor beside him. As he worked, his spectacles slowly slipped down his nose, so he stopped from time to time to push them back up.

After his examination, Doctor Michaels stood up straight and stared down at the threadbare rug beneath his shiny shoes. He sighed heavily then took off his spectacles and rubbed the bridge of his nose.

'It could be some kind of flu,' he said. 'But I don't think so. I've seen something like this before – in my days at Newcastle.' He looked across at Nisha, then back at Mrs F. 'I believe they travelled from Malaya?'

'Yes,' Nisha said, but Doctor Michaels ignored her.

'Well?' he asked the housekeeper. 'Am I right?'

Mrs F glanced at Nisha then back at Doctor Michaels. 'Em, aye. Aye, that's where they've come from.'

'I thought so. Did you know that malaria is rife over there? All the mosquitoes, you see.'

'She had it before,' Nisha said quietly.

'They use quinine to prevent it,' Doctor Michaels went on. 'It comes from the cinchona tree. They even put it in tonic water as a preventative so that—'

'She had it before.' Nisha forced herself to speak louder.

This time Doctor Michaels couldn't ignore her. 'I beg your pardon?'

'I said "she had it before". Malaria.'

Doctor Michaels peered down his nose at Nisha. 'Hm. That would explain a lot. You see, malaria can be treated but sometimes it doesn't go away completely. If you don't get rid of the parasite . . . well, the fever can come back.'

The thought of it was like an icicle in Nisha's soul. She remembered when Amma was first ill with malaria. The fever lasted for weeks and she had almost died.

Doctor Michaels's expression softened and he took a deep breath. He glanced at Mrs F, then forced a smile. 'The fever will pass after time, but she'll need careful attention. I'll send for the right medication.'

'So, you see.' Mrs F came forward and took Nisha's hands. 'She'll be right as rain before you knaa it.'

But the way she said it – she didn't sound as if she really believed it.

Nisha wanted to stay with Amma, but Mrs F said she should leave her to rest. She told Nisha it wasn't healthy to spend too much time in the room with Amma, and that she needed to build up her strength, so she took her downstairs for breakfast.

Nisha would have preferred to eat in the cosy kitchen, but instead she had to go to the cold dining room and sit at one end of a long table. Her grandmother was at the opposite end, eating toast. She didn't even look up when Mrs Foster showed Nisha in.

As Nisha sat down, Mrs F went to speak a few words in Mrs Barrow's ear, then she came back to Nisha.

'I'll bring you an egg,' she said quietly before leaving Nisha alone with her grandmother.

The room was silent except for the crunching of toast and the ticking of the clock on the wall. A large brass pendulum swung backwards and forwards.

Tick-tock.

'Good morning, Grandmother,' Nisha offered.

Mrs Barrow peered down the table at her. 'I'd prefer you to call me "Mrs Barrow" if you don't mind.'

Nisha nodded and lowered her eyes.

The two of them sat in silence until Mrs F returned a few minutes later and put a boiled egg and a single slice of toast in front of Nisha.

The egg was cooked to perfection. Exactly how Amma

made them at home.

'So it's malaria is it?' Mrs Barrow said, taking Nisha by surprise. 'Well, I suppose that's what you get when you live in an uncivilized place. Why Charles had to go and live out there is beyond me. Why he couldn't have stayed here and married a decent English girl, I'll never know.'

Nisha suddenly felt like she was the size of an ant, and even less important. She wanted to crawl into a hole and disappear. That didn't happen though. Instead she had to endure a full five minutes while Mrs Barrow finished her breakfast.

Nisha kept her eyes down, only looking up to check the time on the noisy clock.

Tick-tock.

Finally, Mrs Barrow rose from the table, snapped her napkin, and dropped it beside her plate. Her heels thumped on the worn-out carpet as she crossed the room towards the door. She was wearing heavy brown shoes, similar to the ones the sergeant major wore when he came to the club on backgammon night. Thinking about that brought a sudden flood of comforting memories. Warm evenings filled with laughter and the scent of jasmine. The sound of cicadas crick-cricking in the bamboo around the swimming pool. Sometimes Nisha would even manage to catch one, and would make the insect buzz just by touching its abdomen.

Mrs Barrow stopped with her hand on the doorknob. Without turning around, she said, 'Why was my son not on your ship? How is it that you have reached Barrow Island in one piece but I have heard nothing from your father?'

The happy memories whipped away like a curtain. Reality flooded in like harsh white light and Nisha fought to bite back her tears. Her breath caught in her chest when she remembered what had happened. She felt the terror all over again. Fire and water everywhere. Guilt and horror.

'I . . . The ship . . .' Trying to say it aloud burnt a hole in Nisha's heart. The words refused to form in her mouth. Her face crumpled and tears came in a torrent, flooding out of her. Even her nose ran, which she hated.

Through her tears, Nisha heard the sound of Mrs Barrow's footsteps returning to the table. A handkerchief dropped beside her plate, then the footsteps retreated to the door.

'Try not to get under anyone's feet,' Mrs Barrow said. And with that she was gone.

Extract from Nisha Barrow's Truth, 1942

I thought something was wrong as soon as I saw Papa's car. He almost never came home before lunchtime, and his car was going really fast along the main road through the rubber plantation. And when I saw that Papa was driving instead of Ali, I knew something was wrong because Ali has been Papa's driver for ever, and he always drives Papa, even at weekends. I was on the grass under the jambu tree in front of the bungalow, playing jacks with my painted stones. The sun was shining and the tree was full of pink and red fruit so the warm shade underneath smelt sweet. Amma was inside, drinking tea and playing mahjong with the other ladies, and everything was perfect. The last perfect moment before Papa came driving fast down the road.

After that everything changed.

Amma must have heard Papa's car skidding on the dried palm kernels that cover our driveway because she came out and stood on the step.

Mrs Young came out behind her and said something that made everyone look very nervous and scared.

She said, 'They're coming, aren't they?'

It was two days before Christmas.

10
PAPA'S BOOTS

After breakfast, Nisha went straight up to be with Amma. She didn't want to be anywhere near her grandmother. Grandmothers were supposed to be loving and comforting, but Mrs Barrow was like a cold, hard stone.

Mrs F sat in the armchair in the corner of the bedroom, mending the hole in the elbow of a woolly jumper. She was using the wrong coloured wool.

Nisha perched on the edge of the bed and watched Amma. She couldn't bear to see her so ill. She was afraid she'd lose her as well as Papa, and then she would be alone on this awful island with her beastly grandmother. When tears welled in her eyes, Mrs F sighed.

'Crying's nee use to anyone, pet. There's nowt you can dee for your mam right now, and if you mope about here all day, you'll make yoursel' sick.' She came to sit beside Nisha. 'Mrs Barrow wants you to stay in the house and help with the chores. That's her *orders*. There's always socks to darn and clothes to mend and floors to wash and such-and-such and so-and-so but . . .' She paused. 'What you really need is fresh air and exercise. That's the best medicine for a young 'un that's feeling poorly inside the way you are.'

'I want to stay with Amma.'

'That's the way Mrs Barrow would 'ave it.' Mrs F looked at her old hands for a moment, then spoke quietly. 'Mrs Barrow doesn't want you outside. Even had rules about your fatha playing out when he was a little lad all them years ago. Strict times and places. She'd prefer for you to stay indoors out of trouble, but that's not natural for a young 'un. It wasn't natural for him and it's not natural for you. What you need is sea air to blow away the bad thoughts and make you strong. Trust me, I knaa.'

Nisha shook her head. She turned away from Mrs F and looked at Amma's blood-drained face. It hurt so much to see her like that.

'Your mam'll be just fine,' Mrs F said. 'Doctor Michaels has given her summat for her temperature until he gets the right medication, and he said he'll send someone over from the mainland to help look after her. Jack Donnelly has a whole army of land girls workin' at the farm, and I heard he pays 'em half what he'd pay a man, so I'm sure there's one who'll be willin' to come up to the house for a spell every now and then to earn a few extra shillings. I'll settle it with Mrs Barrow. In the meantime, I'll keep your mam comfy, so all you got to dee is let her rest.'

Mrs F stood up and held out both hands. 'I'm not going to stop you seeing her, but I'll not have you hangin' about here all day neither. I'll set visitin' hours if I must.'

Then the housekeeper leant down, took Nisha's hands in her own, and pulled her to her feet.

'Follow me. Your mam'll still be here when you come back with a clear head and some fresh air inside you.'

As Mrs F said it, the wind picked up outside, as if anticipating Nisha's company. It buffeted the seaward side of Barrow House. The house moaned and the ill-fitting sash windows rattled in their frames. Nisha felt a deep chill pass through her and an image swam into her mind: she saw herself standing on the crag, with the cold wind plucking the dark and confused thoughts from her head and casting them out to sea as if they were painful splinters finally removed. Nisha could almost feel the relief and she suddenly had a strong sense that Mrs F was right. She needed fresh air. She needed to be out of this room and out of this house.

Nisha followed Mrs Foster downstairs to the reception hall where she opened a door close to the main entrance. A faint smell of musty feet wafted out. When Nisha peered inside, she understood why. The small, cold room was filled with shoes and boots. Some were so old, Nisha thought they might have belonged to her great-great-*great* grandparents.

Above them, a row of coats hung from hooks on the wall.

Mrs F passed Nisha her coat, then searched the rows of boots. 'I've got just the thing for you,' she said. 'Where is . . . ah, here we are.'

When she turned to Nisha, Mrs F was holding a pair of boots that looked as if they were no more than a couple of sizes too big for her. The black leather was cracked and creased, and the heels were half worn down.

'These used to be your fatha's.' A faraway smile crossed Mrs F's lips. 'I remember the day he got 'em and he paraded up and down this hallway like a soldier, listenin' to 'em clickety-clacking on the stones.'

Nisha tried to imagine what Papa would have looked like as a boy. 'They were really his?'

'Aye. Gan on, pet. Try 'em on.'

She sat on the floor stones and tugged the boots over the thick woollen socks Mrs F had left out for her. She tied them as tight as she could, then stood up. They made her feet look enormous.

'Well, they're on the big side, but I can't let you out wi' nee boots. Imagine what Mrs Barrow would say if she caught you runnin' about with bare feet like a common urchin.'

Nisha liked having something that had belonged to Papa. She preferred to have no shoes on her feet at all, but if she was going to have to wear some, then what could be better than these?

'Now remember: Mrs Barrow thinks you should be inside doing ladylike things, so this'll have to be our little secret, all reet? Be on your best behaviour out there, and nee monkey business.'

Nisha nodded, but was vaguely aware that Mrs F had turned the tables on her. She was making it seem like it was Nisha who wanted to escape into the fresh air, when it had actually been Mrs F's idea all along. Now that she was wearing her coat and boots, though, she rather liked the idea of exploring the island. And she couldn't shake that feeling of how good it would be to have the wind blow away all the bad thoughts.

'Now ... there's summat I've been meanin' to say.' Mrs F put a fist to her mouth and frowned. 'And there's nee good way to say it, so I'm just goin' to come out with it.'

Nisha looked up at her.

'I take it "Amma" is your word for Mother?'

'Yes.'

'Well, I think it's best if you just call her "Mother" when Mrs Barrow is around. I reckon that's the way Mrs Barrow would want it, so if you want to stay on her good side . . .' Mrs F sighed.

'I'll try,' Nisha said. 'I just want her to like me.'

'So do I.' Mrs F watched Nisha with a sad look, then suddenly reached out and bundled her into her arms. She hugged Nisha hard, then stood back and cleared her throat. She smoothed down her apron and closed the boot room.

'Well, off you gan.' She ushered Nisha through the front door and on to the drive. 'Remember to stay away from the Keep. And divvent gan near the Weepin' Tree.'

At the mention of the tree, Nisha suddenly remembered what she had seen last night in the storm. It was strange that she hadn't thought about it until now. Almost as if the memory was hiding from her.

II

ISLAND EXPLORATION

Nisha stood in front of the house and pulled at the collar of her dress. She was used to colourful cotton clothes that were light and soft, not dark and heavy wool that scratched her skin. She stretched her neck away from the uncomfortable material, but it was no good. It itched worse than the rice sacks that brushed against her bare legs in the storeroom at home. Frustrated, she gave up and tried to ignore it. She watched the island instead, but everything was so dreary.

If she were standing in front of her house in Malaya, the morning sun would be clear in the sky. The air would be warm and fragrant. Along the drive, golden hibiscus flowers would shine with last night's rain, and birds of paradise would bloom among them in bursts of orange and purple. A sunbird would pass from flower to flower, its busy wings a blur of shimmering emerald. Scarlet minivets would play in the tops of the palms that lined the road, and Nisha would slip beneath the shade of her favourite jambu tree to watch the plantation come to life.

On Barrow Island, the morning was cold and damp and flecked with rain. Ugly and brutish gulls squawked in the grey sky, drifting and circling with their wings spread wide. Their mournful cries made Nisha wonder if they were sad too.

The wind blustered, lifting her hair and flicking it about her face, Strands caught on her lips and she pulled them away as she followed the drive around the house.

Papa's boots crunched on the gravel.

Nisha inspected the building as she went, craning her neck to look up at the high windows. She glanced into rooms she had never entered, and tried to imagine Papa playing here when he was her age. It was so alien to her. She couldn't understand how anyone could have fun here.

Without thinking, she slipped her hand into her coat pocket and curled her fingers around the red stone. Her little piece of home.

The drive led around the house and disappeared through an archway into a grey stone courtyard embraced by stables and a small coach house. Chickens scratched in the straw strewn across the stones. Nisha didn't investigate. She would leave that for another day. Instead, she headed for the eastern side of the island, behind the house, where the terrain was more difficult. There were rocky hillocks covered with long yellow grass, and deep troughs filled with wet mud. Nisha was careful to watch her step, but she enjoyed the effort of climbing and looking for the next secure foothold. The exercise helped to clear her mind.

Reaching the top of one particularly high hillock, she saw that the route ahead was blocked by dense bushes. They bristled with needle-like leaves and bloomed with a million faded yellow flowers. The island sucked the colour from them as if it didn't want them to live. Spiny weeds tangled and coiled among them, making the way ahead impenetrable.

Nisha stopped and scanned what she could see of the island from the top of the hillock. Mostly it was bristling bushes and rock. To her right, the sea churned, but further ahead was a large walled area. Nestled in a flat depression in the island, it wouldn't be visible from the ground floor of the house. Nisha guessed it was the same thing she had spotted from the bedroom window last night.

Nisha decided she wanted to investigate, but knew she would have to retrace her steps and find a way around because the spiky bushes were too dense and hostile for her to press on. Looking again, though, she saw a route she hadn't noticed before. As if it had opened up especially for her. The wind pushed at her back, urging her onwards. Nisha pulled her coat tight and headed along the almost invisible path.

The wall was at least three times Nisha's height, and was built from the same grey stone as everything else. Nettles grew around the base, and ivy clung to it; dull green leaves quivering in the wind. Damp yellow moss lived between the cracks.

Nisha put out her hand to touch the rough stone. She leant back to see the ivy creeping to the top and curling over the edges. Running her fingers along the wall, she followed it until she found a rough but well-trodden path that led from the courtyard behind Barrow House all the way to an arched doorway in the wall.

The old wooden door was shut, and there was a large keyhole close to the latch. Nisha expected it to be locked, but when she put her thumb on the latch and pushed, the door clicked open. It didn't move far before it caught on something, so Nisha put her shoulder against it and shoved hard.

The door gave way and swung inwards to reveal a garden bigger than Nisha would have imagined.

Along either side was a line of naked trees. There were

shrubs laid out in rows, some green and living, others still waiting for spring. One area was given over to raised beds edged with heavy wood, the soil turned as if ready for planting. Some were covered with cracked glass, and there were rows of long sticks arranged into tepees. Close to the door, a spade and fork leant against the wall beside a wheelbarrow as if they had been there since the beginning of time.

Nisha stepped into the sheltered garden and closed the door. The wind died behind her. Still with her hand in her pocket, clutching the red stone, she stepped lightly along the stone path. As she did so, she looked down at Papa's boots and wondered how many times they had walked here.

The far end of the garden was a flurry of green. Ivy covered the wall, leaving not a single patch of grey. But as Nisha came closer, she noticed a half-covered archway leading into another, more secluded part of the garden. There was something in there – some kind of structure – but she couldn't quite tell what it was.

Intrigued, Nisha went closer.

12

THE SHELTERED GARDEN

Stepping through the archway into the secluded garden was like stepping away from Barrow Island.

The beds were bursting with flowers of all colours. There were bright pinks, and yellows and reds. Mosaics of flowers all shades of purple. The tidy paths were lined with forests of the tiniest white flowers like tears weeping from green stalks. Criss-cross trellises were crawling with vines sprouting flowers that reminded Nisha of the orchids growing along the drive at home in Malaya. Black birds with bright yellow beaks played among the shrubs and hopped between the flowers. A cheeky robin with an orange-red chest fluttered in an ornate birdbath that stood in the centre of the garden. A pair of plump birds, black and white like the magpie-robins on the plantation, tussled on the grass verges between the flower beds. Seeing them reminded Nisha of trekking into the forest with Papa; his bird book in his pocket, his binoculars around his neck.

Best of all about the garden, though, was the smell. For the first time since arriving on the island, Nisha could breathe something other than the sickening brine of the sea or the stale and musty scent of Barrow House.

Nisha was light on her feet as she glided to the centre of the garden where two paths crossed. Despite the hopelessness of Papa's absence and Amma's illness, she felt a glimmer of warmth in her heart as she circled the birdbath, running her fingers along the edge of the sandy-coloured bowl.

But the structure that most interested her – the one she had seen through the archway – was against the western wall of the secluded garden. Four stone columns stood around a circular stone platform with three shallow steps leading up to it. An ornate dome stretched over the top. Beneath the dome, in the centre of the platform, was a wooden bench.

The perfect place to be alone.

Nisha made her way over to the bench but as she was about to sit down, she noticed a plaque set into one of the columns. Made of black marble, it glinted in the light and was clear of all moss and dirt. Any ivy that had come near it was cut away.

There were words carved into the plaque, inlaid with gold.

IN LOVING MEMORY OF
ELIZABETH BARROW

Nisha read and reread the words, wondering who Elizabeth Barrow was. 'In loving memory' probably meant that she wasn't alive any more, so perhaps she was an old relative. Maybe a great-grandmother or a great-aunt, although Nisha wasn't exactly sure what a great-aunt was. Whoever she was, if she'd been anything like Nisha's grandmother, then Nisha was glad she wasn't here right now. She wouldn't have been able to cope with two bad-tempered old women.

Nisha stopped and told herself not to think such bad thoughts. 'Bad things happen to people who have bad thoughts' was what Amma always said, so she quietly wished Elizabeth Barrow the best of best wishes, then straightened her coat, and sat down.

She pulled at the collar of her itchy dress before taking the red stone from her pocket and holding it tight in her fist.

Sitting there among the flowers, Nisha felt the world outside fade away to dust. For a moment she forgot about Papa left behind in the middle of an invasion. She forgot about Amma shivering and sweating with fever. She forgot about the awfulness of Barrow House and her vile grandmother.

Here, protected from the violent winds that ravaged the island, there were just flowers and the gentle air. She closed her eyes and thought this would be the perfect spot to sit and read a book; just like she used to at home, beneath the jambu tree, listening to the birds in the coconut palms.

Except that was more difficult now because of what had happened. Since the docks in Singapore, she hadn't been able to hear at all from her right ear, and not very well from her left. Everything was muffled now. The bad thought slipped into her head like an unwanted insect. It scuttled over her memories, seeking out the darkest ones and dragging them into the light. And then it all came flooding over her in a wave of dirty water. The hurried escape from home. The chaos of evacuation. The screams and the crying and the ugly fate of a boy called David Hill.

Amma had told her to think good thoughts when the bad ones came. She had told her to imagine a good place, a good time, but it was so hard to stop the unwanted pictures. It was impossible to—

The air grew dreadfully still. A deep chill passed through her and something cold lay gently across Nisha's hand. An unexpected dry weight on her skin. For an instant there was a distinct sense that someone was sitting beside her and she felt icy breath in her ear.

Nisha's eyes flicked open. She sat upright and pushed herself against the back of the bench, raising her hands to protect herself, but there was no one there. She was alone.

Then, from the corner of her eye, she caught sight of movement and turned just in time to see a skinny boy disappear behind a trellis at the north end of the garden.

13

THE OVERGROWN PATH

Nisha was on her feet in an instant.

Jumping down the steps, she raced along the path and leapt over a bed of blushing pink flowers. She dodged around a collection of shrubs, moving as quickly as she could, but when she finally reached the trellis and looked behind it, there was no sign of the boy.

Nisha was weak from the long and difficult journey to England, so the effort of running had made her light-headed. She was breathing hard, and the cold air was harsh in her throat. She stood with her fists on her hips as she caught her breath, wondering where the boy had disappeared to. And was he the same boy she had seen yesterday? Beneath the tree? He had to be, but who was he? And why had Mrs F said there was no one else on the island?

Perhaps he was an intruder. Perhaps no one else knew he was here. Or perhaps there was a secret on Barrow Island.

A rustling in the ivy that covered the outer wall of the garden caught her attention. She crept closer, half expecting someone to peer out from the dense creepers.

She had the strangest feeling that someone was watching her. It was an eerie tingle at the back of her neck, but when she looked around, the garden was empty except for the birds and the flowers. All she could hear was the hush of the wind and the crash of the sea beyond the garden.

'Are you watching me?' she whispered to the two black-and-white birds now perched on top of the ornate dome.

They chattered in reply.

Nisha turned back to the wall and peered closer, catching sight of something behind the deep green leaves. She reached out with one hand and pushed the trailing creepers aside to reveal a door-sized hole in the wall. There were hinges in the stone, where a gate had once been fixed but was now gone. Leading away from the doorway was a rocky path half reclaimed by the island. Overgrown with grass and brambles, the path climbed towards the clifftop where it split like a serpent's tongue. One route cut straight up to the ruined Keep that over-looked the sea. The other curved towards the Weeping Tree that stood close by on the crag.

There was no sign of the boy.

The wind picked up and hissed through the thick and spiky bushes that grew over the path from both sides. It whispered to her, enticing her towards the crag.

Nisha couldn't take her eyes off the tree. She was close enough now to see the twisted branches spreading outwards and upwards from the thick, knotted trunk. And in the palm of that dead-looking claw was a tree house that must have once been splendid. But now the white paint was cracked and peeling, the windows were shattered, and the roof was thick with moss. The decaying building leant to one side so that one end hung directly over the long drop to the sea below.

Down and down into the dark.

The wind curled around her. Nisha felt as if she were neither awake nor asleep. The sting of the salt air was gone. The crash of waves had faded. The emptiness of her loss had disappeared. It was the strangest feeling; as if she were no longer on the crag but had slipped into a place between worlds where —

A harsh cough startled her back to Barrow Island.

Nisha blinked and looked around to see that she was no longer standing by the wall. Without realizing it, she had stepped through the hidden doorway and was making her way along the overgrown path. She was already more than halfway along it. Standing in an ocean of long grass and thorny bushes, she was almost at the top of the crag. The Weeping Tree was just ahead, with the tree house jutting out over the edge of the crag. And beyond it, the grey waves of the North Sea crashed over the rocks far below.

Nisha had been told not to go near the tree. It was forbidden. A rule of the island. But the tree had drawn her to it. Nisha hadn't been afraid. Not really. She felt as if she *should* have been afraid, but something about the tree had comforted her. Nevertheless, she was confused to find herself so close to it without really remembering how she had got there. And, more than anything, she was worried she would be seen breaking the rules. So she turned and hurried back to the hidden doorway. Brambles snagged at her coat and dress.

When she reached the wall and pushed back through the ivy, Nisha saw her grandmother enter the flower garden from the far side.

Immediately, Nisha ducked out of sight and parted the leaves just enough to watch her grandmother walk to the birdbath where she stood for a while, just staring. She was wearing a coarse tweed skirt and jacket, and the same stout shoes she had been wearing earlier.

After a moment, Nisha's grandmother approached

the stone structure. When she reached it, she stopped and stood as if she were praying – the way Amma did in front of her small shrine in the bedroom every morning. Then she climbed the steps and sat down on the bench.

She sat exactly where Nisha had been sitting earlier, when she had felt that strange cold touch on her skin.

Was it him? she thought with a shiver. *Did that boy touch my hand?*

Nisha watched her grandmother take a handkerchief from her pocket and wipe her eyes.

That was when Nisha realized her grandmother was crying.

I've never seen Papa look like he did on the day we escaped from the plantation. There was that one time when we were at the Thursday market (which Amma calls 'crowded chaos') and I got lost but this was much worse. When he came racing up the drive and jumped out of the car, he looked _really_ scared. The ladies were all on the step and I could tell they were scared too – even before Papa said anything. And then he told us 'they' were just fifteen miles away, and all of a sudden everything was a muddle of people talking all at once, and that was the end of everything.

The invasion started two weeks before. The Japanese attacked Kota Bharu and there was a big fight. Everyone said the Japanese were rubbish soldiers with nothing but bicycles so the British would keep them back easily. Everyone said there was nothing to be afraid of. But they were wrong. They were wrong about a lot of things. Adults often are, I think, even though they act as if they know everything. And now the Japanese were just fifteen miles away from the rubber plantation and we heard a thump in the distance that was like a short crack of thunder, or something clattering in the factory. A lorry crash, even.

It was a bomb, though. I know that now. A horrible, horrible bomb, and after that everything went quiet. Everything just stopped. The soft shouts from the factory. Cars on the road. Birds singing. The breeze in the palms. Even the cicadas stopped making that crick-crick-crick noise, and then we heard planes flying right into the hole-of-no-sound.

Amma was about to take me back into the house but Papa stopped her.

'The tree!' he shouted. 'Everyone into the tree!'

The banyan tree is right there by the veranda. It's more than a hundred years old and stronger than any house could ever be. All those vines hanging down and planting themselves to make new trunks make it look like a whole forest of its own. In some places it's so thick even the light can't get through. Seti and Dewi call it pokok hantu because that means ghost tree, and it's where the ghosts live. The hantu. They live right in the heart of the tree and it's not just Seti and Dewi who say the hantu live there – all the Malays say it. They <u>all</u> believe in hantu. Some of the children, like Suraya, wear black silk around their wrist to protect them. They won't even go close to the tree and they say it's bad luck to cut it down.

I told them not to be so silly, that there are no such thing as ghosts because that's what Papa says but they just shook their heads as if I know nothing. And I always kept away from the tree just in case. Because no one really knows for sure, do they?

Sometimes I sat on the veranda, watching the tree through the mosquito netting trying to see the ghosts, but Seti and Dewi said that if I looked at the tree for too long the ghosts would know I was there and come to get me. There's definitely something dangerous about it. The way it smells. The darkness in its forest of trunks and vines. And whenever I was near it, I always felt like Seti and Dewi might be right. Maybe it really is where the ghosts live.

But on the day the planes came, the banyan tree was the safest place for us.

14

A MOMENT OF JOY

Nisha's experience on the overgrown path meant she was keen to stay away from the Weeping Tree. She felt her gaze drawn to it time and time again, but that part of the island was forbidden. She didn't want to give her grandmother any more reasons to hate her, so she decided to explore the opposite side of the island that afternoon.

She was standing on the dunes looking across at the mainland when she saw two figures cycling across the causeway. As they came closer, Nisha recognized the black coat and hat that Doctor Michaels had been wearing that morning. The other cyclist was a woman.

Nisha remembered that Mrs F had mentioned a 'land girl' might come to help, though she had no idea what a 'land girl' might be.

Whoever it was, if she was going to look after Amma, it seemed proper that Nisha should meet her.

When Nisha made it back to the house, Doctor Michaels was already in the bedroom, beside Amma's bed.

'. . . doesn't seem any better,' he was muttering as Nisha came in. 'I'm doing everything I can but I don't have the right medication yet. Antimalarials are so hard to come by. They're all being directed to the troops overseas. It's just so difficult to get what I need with this damn war going on for—'

Mrs F cleared her throat loudly. 'Nisha, pet. Doctor Michaels was just sayin' these things often get worse before they get better, isn't that right Doctor Michaels?'

'What? Oh. Umm. Yes, it certainly is.' He took off his glasses and rubbed the bridge of his nose. 'It certainly is.' He looked at Nisha as if he were trying to remember who she was.

Nisha's attention was drawn to the young woman standing close to the armchair in the corner of the room.

'You must be Nisha.' She came forward with a friendly smile and a light step. 'I'm Joy. I'll be looking after your mam from time to time, to give Mrs F a break. Evenings mostly, and night-time, depending on the tides. I have to tell you, though, I've been dying to meet you.'

Nisha raised a hand to greet her, but Joy ignored it. Instead, she put her arms around Nisha and pulled her tight so that their cheeks touched. She smelt like flowers and fresh air and Lifebuoy soap.

'You've come such a long way,' Joy said. 'All the way from Malaya! How exciting! I don't even know where that is, but I want to hear all about it. You must tell me everything.' She moved back and held Nisha at arm's length to take a long look at her. 'You're so pretty!'

Joy had bright eyes, and waves of short auburn hair. In her red jacket and skirt, she was a splash of colour and a breath of fresh air in the musty old house.

Nisha knew immediately that they would get along famously.

Eventually Doctor Michaels left, and Mrs F went down to prepare supper, so Nisha stayed with Joy in Amma's room. There was something special about her that made Nisha feel relaxed and comfortable. Perhaps it was her smile, her smell, or the way her voice sounded like music. Perhaps it was the gentle way she cooled Amma's brow with a cloth. Whatever it was, it filled Nisha with warmth, and she found herself talking so much it felt as if her words were falling over each other.

Joy had a million questions, and Nisha answered every single one of them, reliving the happiest moments of her life. Nisha told Joy about the birds and the flowers. She talked about the jungle and what it was like to live on the rubber plantation. Joy was especially excited by the idea that they had an outdoor swimming pool at the club, right beside four tennis courts all in a row.

Joy sat in the armchair, and Nisha on the footstool, watching the smile on Joy's lips, and the kindness that shone in her eyes.

'Mrs Foster said you're a land girl,' Nisha said. 'What does that mean?'

'Ah.' Joy sat up straight and flexed her arm as if she were showing her muscles. 'They need strong girls to work the farms,' she said. 'All the men are away fighting so we have to do their jobs for them. Mind you, Mr Donnelly pays us twenty-eight shillings a week but deducts fourteen for board and lodging. I heard he paid the men thirty-eight shillings and they didn't even work as many hours.'

'That doesn't sound fair,' Nisha said.

'Very true! But I suppose there's a war on so we have to make do. Anyway, I spend most of my time on the farm catching rats. And not just rats. Foxes and rabbits too.'

'Why?'

'To eat.'

'You eat rats?'

'No.' Joy laughed. 'We only eat the rabbits, you silly

goose. I suppose you *could* eat rats and foxes if you had to but . . . No. We have to stop the rats from getting into the stores, and we have to stop the foxes from eating the hens.' She lifted both hands and tilted her head, closing one eye as if she were aiming down the barrel of a gun. 'Mr Donnelly has taught me to use his shotgun. And I'm a crack shot as it happens.'

'Really?'

'Oh aye. So if those nasty Germans try to get on this island, I'll take Mr Donnelly's shotgun and shoot 'em.'

'Do you really think they'll come?' Nisha frowned and looked towards the window. It was dark outside now.

'Oh.' Joy lowered her arms. 'I didn't mean to scare you.'

Nisha looked at her hands. She picked the skin around the edge of her thumbnail.

'It must be difficult for you,' Joy said. 'Coming so far away from home. You must miss it terribly.'

Nisha nodded.

'I heard about the evacuation on the wireless. Those Japanese are as beastly as the Germans, aren't they? Was it awful?'

Nisha didn't answer. She loved talking about home, but there were some things she just didn't want to remember.

15
THE WRONG THING

Nisha ate supper in the dining room, sitting exactly where she had sat at breakfast. Her grandmother was at the opposite end of the table, with her back straight and her nose in the air.

It was dark outside, and the room was barely lit with a dull lamp.

'I expect you think the food is rather drab,' Mrs Barrow said as she moved her spoon through the watery grey soup in her bowl. 'Not like the exotic fare you're accustomed to in the tropics, I suppose.'

Nisha looked up from her bowl to see her grandmother glaring across the table at her.

'There is a war on, you know,' said Mrs Barrow. 'And it's been going on here a lot longer than out there in the sunshine.' She sipped soup from her spoon then dabbed the corner of her mouth with a napkin. It made Nisha remember how her grandmother had dabbed her eyes in the garden earlier that day.

It was unusual to see a grown-up cry. Nisha wondered if the tears had been for Papa. Who else would they be for? And when she really thought about it, she realized that Papa wasn't just her father and Amma's husband. He was also Grandmother's son, and it must have made her very sad to know he was lost. So Nisha decided to be kind, no matter how horrible her grandmother might seem. It was what Amma would have wanted her to do.

'I'm sorry Papa wasn't on the ship with us,' Nisha said.

'So am I.'

'You must miss him.'

Mrs Barrow opened her mouth as if she were about to say something, then she lowered her eyes and sighed. 'Yes, I do. I miss him very much. He and I, we ... didn't always get along as well as we could have done, but he will always be my son.'

They ate in silence for a while, but Nisha felt as if she had made a connection with her grandmother, however small. In Papa, they had something in common. But that wasn't the only thing. There was something else.

'I went to the garden today,' Nisha said.

Mrs Barrow looked up.

'It's very beautiful,' Nisha went on.

'I hope you didn't get in Mr Foster's way.'

'I don't think so,' Nisha said. 'I found the garden at the back.'

Mrs Barrow stopped with her spoon hovering over her bowl. Her lips tightened.

'There's a flower that reminded me of home,' Nisha said. 'Like an orchid but not an orchid.'

Mrs Barrow watched her across the table for a while then said, 'That might be the clematis. There are snow-drops too. The little white flowers.'

'I saw those. They're pretty. But my favourite is the pink one that makes the garden smell so lovely. It's even stronger than the smell of the sea.'

'That'll be the daphne.' When she said it, Mrs Barrow had a faraway look in her eyes. As if she was seeing something that wasn't there. 'That was always her favourite.'

'Whose?' Nisha asked. 'Elizabeth's?'

Mrs Barrow's spoon clattered in her bowl. Soup splashed on to the tablecloth. Her eyes widened and she stared at Nisha.

'I . . .' Nisha realized it was the wrong thing to say before she could stop the words escaping her mouth. '. . . saw the plaque.'

Without a word, Mrs Barrow got to her feet. She stood for a moment, hands trembling, then strode from the dining room.

It was the second time she had left Nisha sitting alone that day.

16

KITCHEN DANCE

'So who *is* Elizabeth Barrow?' Nisha asked Mrs F.
'We divvent mention that name,' said Mrs F.

They were at the enormous table in the kitchen. The cat was settled on Nisha's lap while she watched Mrs F rubbing eggs with lard to keep them fresh.

'I didn't mean to make her angry,' Nisha said.

'No one ever does, but y'know, there was a time she had such a laugh on her? Now she barely even cracks a smile.'

Nisha watched Mrs F to see if she was joking. She couldn't imagine her grandmother laughing about anything.

'I reckon that's what drove your fatha all the way across to the other side of the world,' Mrs F went on.

'What happened?'

'None of your beeswax. Divvent ask again.'

Nisha sighed. 'How's Amma? Can I go up and see her now?'

'She's resting, so best leave her a while longer. Joy's keeping an eye on her.'

That's all Mrs F would say – that Amma was 'resting' – but the sad looks she kept giving her made Nisha think things might be worse than Mrs F was letting on.

'*Please*?' Nisha asked.

'Tell you what; I'll put the wireless on, eh? There's usually something on round about now.'

Mrs F turned the dial and the wireless crackled into life. The reception was only just good enough on the island.

'Oh, I love this tune!' Joy waltzed into the kitchen. '"In the Mood" by The Four King Sisters.'

'You're supposed to be upstairs.' Mrs F glared at her.

'I just came down for a cup of hot water.' Joy twirled around the table and danced close to Mrs F. 'Unless you can spare a few leaves?'

'I'll find you some nettles.'

'I was hoping for tea,' Joy smiled.

'I'll send you upstairs with nowt but an empty cup if you're not careful, you cheeky young thing,' Mrs F warned, but she couldn't help smiling when Joy took one of Mrs F's hands and wrapped an arm around her waist.

'Dance with me, Mrs F. You know you want to.'

Nisha watched the two of them dance a couple of graceful twirls around the kitchen table. Mrs F was surprisingly light on her feet, and she had such a smile on her face that, for a moment, Nisha forgot all her troubles. With the cat purring on her lap, and Joy brightening the room like sunshine, it was as if nothing was wrong in the world.

And when Mrs F broke away and smoothed out her apron, pretending to disapprove of Joy's manner, Joy took Nisha by the hand and danced her once around the kitchen.

The cat wasn't pleased, but it lifted Nisha's spirits.

'You're an excellent dancer,' Joy said when she paused from humming along with the tune. 'I'd dance the night away with you. Where did you learn?'

'On the plantation,' Nisha said. 'There were dances and parties all the time. Sometimes until very late at night.' She remembered listening to the music when she was supposed to be asleep, or sneaking out of bed, the tiles cool on her bare feet while she watched the dancing figures.

'That sounds wonderful,' Joy said. 'I think I'd like to live in Malaya when the war is over.'

Before the tune had even ended, though, Mrs F

reached for the wireless and turned it off.

'Spoilsport,' Joy said. 'I'd bet Nisha has at least one more dance in her.'

'Shh!' Mrs F cocked her head to one side. 'D'you not hear that?'

Nisha listened as hard as she could, but shook her head.

'You divvent hear that?' Mrs F frowned.

'No.' Nisha turned her head.

'I do.' Joy looked serious. 'Sounds like planes.'

Extract from Nisha Barrow's Truth, 1942

When we heard the planes coming over the plantation, everything felt extra real. The war wasn't just happening in Kota Bharu and in newspapers any more, it was right on top of us. We ran into the shade of the banyan tree and pushed through the curtains of vines to climb between its trunks. The ladies were making scared noises and squashing in wherever they could find space. Some together, some just on their own. No one said anything but I could tell how frightened everyone was and that made me frightened too.

We were all inside when the first bomb hit. I don't know where it hit, but it must have been close because it was _so_ loud. The whole ground shook. Even the banyan tree trembled and insects rained down from the leaves. From where I was crouching, between two thick trunks with my face against the cold bark, I could see through the vines to the veranda. I could even see the table inside and the mahjong set still halfway through a game. When the ground shook, a dark crack ran right up the wall, and then part of the roof caved in. Tiles crashed down on top of the mahjong set and the table broke and there was a big cloud of dust.

There wasn't any screaming. No one made a sound.

It was as if we were hiding from the planes or maybe we were too scared to even breathe, I can't really remember – but I do remember that Amma was behind me and she put her arms around me and held me tight. Papa stood in front of us to protect us, and he stared right at me. I was shaking so much but he smiled at me and whispered, 'Be brave,' but there wasn't really anything anyone could do. It didn't matter if he stood in front of us or if I was the bravest person in the world because if a bomb fell on the tree, we'd all have been dead. The way the ground shook and the veranda cracked in half, I knew even the old banyan tree wouldn't survive the Japanese bombs.

There were more bombs after that, but nothing fell any closer. And then the planes went over and the sound got so loud I thought they must be right on top of us, but a moment later they were gone. We didn't dare move for ages after that. We thought Japanese soldiers might come to kill us so we stayed squashed inside the tree until my legs went numb. Even when a spider crawled across my hand, I didn't move an inch until Papa said it was safe to come out.

No soldiers came, but Papa said the planes were 'preparing the way'. That meant soldiers would be on their way soon enough.

The ladies stumbled out of the tree and on to the drive. Their nice dresses were all dirty and their hair was all messy. Amma was wearing a beautiful sari that got ripped on the tree but I don't think she even noticed.

And then more cars were racing down the main road as the men came to find their wives. We waited while Papa went to talk to some of them. It didn't take long before he came back to us and the cars drove away.

'Pack some clothes,' Papa said to Amma. 'One suitcase, that's all. We have a ship to catch.'

17

SO MUCH HORROR

Mr Foster hurried in from the back of the house through the scullery. He came up the steps and leant his head round the door.

'Bloody planes,' he said. 'We should get you ladies to the shelter. Both Mrs Barrows, too.'

'Well, I knaa what her ladyship will say,' Mrs F told him. 'And Nisha's mam is in nee state to be moved.'

'Planes?' Nisha couldn't hide the fear in her voice.

Mr Foster had left the scullery door open and the wind was blowing in from the courtyard. When Nisha turned her good ear towards it, she felt the cold against her warm face. And carried in the wind was the dull tone of engines.

The sound washed around her, dragging dark memories from hidden depths.

'Is it the Japanese?' Her voice was small. 'Are they coming to get us?'

'Japanese?' Mr Foster said. 'I shouldn't expect so, pet. They would've had to fly a long way to get here. Naa, they'll be Hitler's planes again.'

The noise grew louder and louder until it was everything.

Nisha slipped her hand into her pocket and gripped the stone tight in her fist. She squeezed her eyes shut and backed against the table, hunching her shoulders and trying to make herself disappear.

'We'll be all right.' Joy went to her. 'I promise.'

But Nisha knew it was a promise Joy couldn't keep. She had no control over the planes and the bombs.

'Never fear, pet, they haven't dropped a bomb on us yet.' Mr Foster had to raise his voice. 'And I divvent think they ever will. They've got better things to bomb than our ghostly little island.'

Mrs F gave him a stern look. 'Wisht your talk about bombs and ghosts, Bill Foster.' She grabbed Nisha's hand and pulled her close. 'You stay with me, pet. Joy, gan upstairs and check on the other Mrs Barrow.'

Joy hesitated as she looked at Nisha, then saluted, 'Aye aye captain,' and hurried out.

Nisha's muscles cramped and her chest tightened.

Suddenly she could hardly draw breath, and an awful sickness rose up into her throat. But if Mrs F noticed, she didn't say anything. She just took up a lamp and dragged Nisha out of the kitchen. They flew along the passageway and across the entrance hall to knock on the study door.

'If it's about those damn planes, I don't want to know!' came the reply from Nisha's grandmother.

'They're gettin' close,' said Mrs F. 'Should we get to the shelter just in case?'

'I'll not be chased from my house by foreigners! I've told you before and I shan't tell you again, I'll not move for those foreigners.'

'Well?' Joy leant over the balustrade, holding a lamp. The planes were so loud she had to shout. 'Are we going to the shelter? I'll need help to bring Mrs Barrow down.'

The noise was unbearable. The planes *had* to be right over them because the whole house was trembling. The doors were shaking and the paintings were rattling against the walls.

'I think it's too late anyway,' Mrs F yelled as she pointed at the ceiling. 'They'll be gone over by the time we get there.'

She was right. It was only a few more seconds before the world-shaking noise softened and the planes passed beyond the island. A moment longer and it was nothing more than a gentle hum.

'Maybe we should get to the shelter anyway,' Joy said,

lowering her voice. 'You know they sometimes drop bombs on the way back if they've got any left. There was one dropped on—'

Mrs F stopped her when she felt Nisha's hand tighten in her own. 'They won't be dropping bombs on Barrow Island. Not tonight. Not *ever*. Now, gan and sit with Mrs Barrow and I'll bring you up a cup of tea.'

'And a biscuit?' Joy suggested.

'I've got mashed swede if you'd like a scoop of that? Or a lump of tripe?'

'Ugh. Thanks, but no thanks! Tea will be enough.' Joy withdrew from the balustrade and disappeared.

'She's a funny onion, that 'un,' said Mrs F as she led Nisha back to the kitchen where Mr Foster was waiting for them.

'Divvent worry,' he said when he saw the look on Nisha's face. 'They've gone over now. Why don't you come and look?' He headed down into the scullery.

'I don't want to.' Nisha shook her head and tried to pull away.

'It's all reet, pet, it'll be excitin'. Howay.' Mrs F kept hold of her hand as she took Nisha down into the scullery where the door to the courtyard was wide open.

'I don't want to.' Nisha stopped in the doorway. Her breath was like steam in the cold night.

'Come along.' Mrs F encouraged her out into the courtyard. 'You've nothing to be scared of now.'

There were lights in the distance. Five or six great white beams pointed up at the sky. They illuminated the low clouds, casting plane-shaped shadows in the heavens. Tiny explosions erupted around them like fireflies dancing at the edge of the jungle. Below, the land flickered with violent flashes of white and orange. Even with her poor hearing, Nisha could hear the booms and thuds.

'I don't want to.' She cringed, and hunched her shoulders. 'Please.'

'It's all reet, pet.'

'I can't.' Nisha was starting to panic. It was all flooding back to her now: planes diving from the sky; the stink of burning rubber and petrol; the drowning sea; the face of a boy called David Hill.

And horror. So much horror.

She had to get away from it.

She had to escape.

18

SOMETHING BAD

Nisha tugged her hand from Mrs F's and blundered back into the house.

Mrs F called after her, but Nisha ran blindly through the scullery, and into the kitchen. She hardly even knew where she was going as she pushed through the door, raced along the passageway, and up the stairs in almost total darkness. She somehow managed to find her way to Amma's room and barged straight in.

Joy was on her feet in a second. Her book fell from her lap to land – *thump* – on the floor. A lamp flickered on the table beside her.

'What's going on?' she said as Nisha rushed in and

threw herself on the bed, burying herself against Amma.

Amma managed to mumble Nisha's name but didn't have the strength for anything more.

'What happened?' Joy went to her. 'Did something happen?'

Before she could ask again, Mrs F came in, bringing the orange glow of another lamp. 'What on earth's got into you?' she panted. 'What's the matter?'

Nisha's whole body was shaking and she was struggling to take a proper breath.

'Come along.' Mrs F gently tried to sit her up. 'Your mam needs to rest, and you divvent need to be so scared. You'll get used to the planes.'

Nisha drew away from her, pushing harder against Amma.

When Mrs F tried again, Joy stopped her. 'It's all right,' she said. 'You do what you need to do and I'll look after Nisha. She can stay here a while, and when she's ready, I'll see she gets to bed.'

'She's my responsibility,' said Mrs F. 'I should—'

'I don't mind.' Joy's tone was soft and understanding. 'I have a brother at home who's about Nisha's age, so I know what I'm doing. We'll be fine.'

Mrs F thought about it for a moment then sighed. 'All reet. Thank you.'

As she was about to leave, she stopped by the door and looked back. 'Goodnight and . . .'

'Yes?'

'Keep her safe.'

Joy smiled. 'I will.'

Nisha was still trembling when the planes returned. They grew louder as they passed the island, then they turned and headed out to sea.

'Back over to Norway,' Joy said. 'We're all safe and sound now, no harm done.'

It was quiet in the bedroom for a long while after that. Joy made no attempt to stop Nisha from being with Amma. She just sat in the chair and read her book.

Nisha lay beside Amma, listening to her breathing until she eventually looked over at Joy.

'Is she going to be all right?' she asked.

'I honestly don't know.' Joy lowered her book. 'Doctor Michaels said these things sometimes get worse before they get better.' She closed the book and put it on the table beside her. 'Why don't we see if we can make her more comfortable?'

Nisha eased away from Amma and helped adjust the covers and pillow. She then sat on the edge of the bed while Joy soaked a cloth in a bowl of cool water and wrung it out.

'She's very beautiful,' Joy said as she dabbed Amma's brow with the cloth. 'And I bet she's a fabulous person.'

'She is.' Nisha put a hand on Amma's arm.

'We'll look after her,' said Joy. 'Don't you worry.' She dabbed Amma's forehead again. 'The planes scared you, didn't they?'

'Mm-hm.'

'Have you ever seen anything like that before?'

Nisha shrugged.

'Did something happen to you? Something bad?'

Nisha started picking at the skin around her thumbnail. She pulled up a small flap of skin that she nibbled off with her front teeth.

'Did you know that I want to be a nurse?' Joy said. 'Did they tell you that?'

'No.'

'It's true. I applied to the hospital in Newcastle but I haven't heard from them yet. I've learnt a thing or two, though. For example, I know that it can help to talk about things that are bothering you. Everyone tries to put on a brave face these days, but it's all right to be sad, you know. And it's all right to say you're sad, or angry, or not feeling good. Bottling everything up can make you feel worse and . . . well, if you need to talk to someone, I'm a good listener.'

Nisha looked up at her.

'Not as good as I am at dancing,' Joy said, 'but pretty good.'

Nisha laughed, and a little bit of snot came out of her nose. That made Joy laugh and call her a 'silly goose', and then Nisha laughed even harder.

Extract from Nisha Barrow's Truth, 1942

We left the plantation just before lunchtime on the first day of the bombs. All I had was my little suitcase with some clothes and a toothbrush. Not any of my toys except for my best jacks stone that I found when we went for a picnic at the river that runs through the rubber trees. It was my thirteenth birthday and Dewi made nasi bungkus with banana leaves wrapped around them so they were like emeralds. And inside, the rice was just sticky enough and the filling was just spicy enough (I wish I had some now!). We also had juicy satays with peanut sauce and Amma made crispy samosas with green chutney. There was fresh pineapple too. And then we swam in the river and the water was freezing cold and the current was strong. Amma had the idea to collect stones to play jacks. When we got home Seti helped me paint them different colours. Blue and green and red and white.

But the red one was always my favourite.

After the bombs and hiding in the banyan tree everyone was going to Singapore. They said the Japanese were getting closer every minute. A man on the wireless said there were ships in Singapore, and that they were taking people away to where it was safe. Papa said he knew a chap who would get us on a ship, so that's where we should go. Papa said we had to be brave and that we would be all right. I said I didn't feel brave and that I had been scared when we were hiding in the banyan tree and Papa said he was scared too. Then he told me that being brave isn't being not scared. It's being scared but finding a way to carry on. 'Courage is conquering fear.' Funny how I remember it exactly the way he said it. 'Courage is conquering fear.' As if it's something you can fight. I think about that a lot because I'm always scared and I don't ever feel brave.

I knelt on the back seat of the car as we drove away, and I looked back at the bungalow with the veranda roof all caved in. Dewi and Seti were standing at the front door. Dewi had looked after me ever since I was a little baby and I wish she was here now because she would know how to make Amma better and she's much nicer than my grandmother.

Seti looked after the house but most of all he made me laugh — especially when he turned his songkok hat sideways and made funny faces. Or when he put his shirt on and the hanger was still in it. The best thing was sitting with Dewi and Seti at the back of the house eating plain rice with our fingers. Sometimes Seti would catch the geckos off the wall and show me how their tails come off and wriggle about in the palm of your hand. But it's all right because the tails grow back.

Dewi was crying when we left, but I wasn't because I thought we'd be back as soon as it was safe. I don't think that any more. I don't think it will ever be safe again, and I don't think I'll ever see Dewi and Seti again. Instead, I'll have to live with my ghastly grandmother on this awful grey island for the rest of my life.

I lie in bed at night and hope they're all right and that the soldiers didn't hurt them, but I think maybe there's no hope left in the world for anything. It's as if someone threw all the hope into the sea and drowned it.

19
HANTU

Nisha wanted to sleep in Amma's room, but Joy thought it was better not to.

'I'll be right next door,' she said. 'If you need me, all you have to do is call.'

Nisha wasn't happy about it, but Joy insisted. 'It's better for you and your mam,' she said. 'You both need a good night's sleep.'

Nisha stood in the passageway and looked into her room. It was dark and cold and unfamiliar. Every corner harboured a nightmare. Every shadow reached for her soul. She remembered the figure in the storm beneath the Weeping Tree last night, the gentle touch on her hand,

and how she had found herself standing on the overgrown path. She thought about the ghosts in the banyan tree at home. Had she looked at the tree for too long? Had the *hantu* followed her here? Were they waiting in the darkness to swallow her?

'Come in with me,' she whispered. 'Help me check.'

'I wouldn't have it any other way, you silly goose. I'm just sorry I can't do anything about the cold – it's bloomin' freezin' in here!' Joy walked in with confidence and the truth of her lamp revealed the monsters for what they really were.

A washstand with a porcelain bowl and jug standing in the corner. A commode and a chest of drawers by the window. A small desk and chair.

'And there's nothing under the bed.' Joy held the lamp close to illuminate the emptiness. 'Not even a spider or a speck of dust. Crikey, Mrs F is thorough!'

They checked the chest of drawers, finding every drawer empty but one.

'Greyhound, The Game of Goose . . .' Joy lifted out a selection of board games in battered, once-colourful boxes. 'There's dominoes in here too. We could play these sometime if you like?'

Nisha nodded.

'Or, better still, one of the girls has Buccaneer. Have you ever played it?'

'No.'

'You'll love it,' she smiled. 'It has its own map and everything. I'll try to remember to bring it next time I come.'

They found some old toys in a chest – wooden cars, a few wind-up soldiers, and more bags of marbles than a person could want. And when they looked in the wardrobe, they discovered that it was full of boys' clothes in different sizes. Shirts and short trousers. A selection of jackets with patched elbows.

Nisha ran her hand along them. The coat hangers rattled, and there was a strong waft of mothballs that reminded her of home.

'These were Papa's,' she said.

'Yes, I suppose that makes sense,' Joy agreed. 'That's nice, isn't it? You'll be sleeping in the room he slept in when he was your age.'

Nisha pulled at the neck of her dress where it was itching. She wondered what would happen if she took one of the shirts for herself. They looked far more comfortable than this awful woollen dress. And they were Papa's. It would make her feel closer to him. Like wearing his boots.

Once Nisha was convinced there was nothing hiding in the room, she changed into her nightclothes. Her teeth chattered in the cold. When she was ready, Joy rubbed her shoulders warm then tucked her up in bed and read a few pages aloud from her book. She even gave Nisha a gentle kiss on the forehead like Amma usually did.

'I'll check on you in the night,' Joy said before she left. 'Make sure you're asleep.'

At times during her voyage to England, the sea had been so rough the whole ship had lurched from side to side. When planes or warships came close, fear had spread from deck to deck, and cabin to cabin like a plague. And whenever someone said they'd seen something unusual in the water, there had been panic that it might be a U-boat lurking beneath the waves.

Amma had taught Nisha that during those dark moments, it was best to remember the good things. Bright mornings and warm days. Peeling fresh rambutans and biting into the soft white fruit. Splashing in the pool with Papa. Sitting in the shade drinking fresh lime juice laced with lashings of brown sugar.

Nisha tried to think about those things while she was lying alone in bed in Barrow House. She tried to imagine having those things again, but in the deep darkness, with the blackout curtain pulled across the window, the light of hope flickered out. The foulest thoughts pushed her happy memories away, and she knew she would never go back.

She curled into a ball, shivering and crying herself to sleep.

*

Sometime during the night, Nisha became aware that she was not alone. Lying on her side, huddled beneath the sheets, she sensed a presence behind her, lurking in the corner of the room. It didn't make a sound but she knew it was there. She could feel it watching her, cold and unnatural. A terrifying stillness polluted the air. And then came the slightest breeze as the presence shifted and slipped silently towards her. Gliding across the floor, it moved as freely as a dream.

Nisha's heart beat faster. Her skin crawled with fear, but she didn't dare move. She didn't dare open her eyes. She didn't even dare to breathe.

The presence stopped at the edge of the bed behind her.

Nisha squeezed her eyes shut and felt a cold breath on her neck.

Soft fingers reached through the blankets, and curled around Nisha's hand.

In that moment, she heard her name as if whispered in the distance, and something coarse brushed her feet and ankles. Then the cold breeze was on her skin and she had the most peculiar feeling. It was as if the bed was whipped out from under her and suddenly she was falling and her eyes opened with a start and—

Nisha was no longer in bed.

20

SILVER TEARS

She was outside. On the overgrown path. The rocky track from the sheltered garden to the crag at the north end of Barrow Island. A cold wind rushed through the bushes, lifting a faint smell of coconut and vanilla from the flowers.

Nisha was wearing her coat over her nightdress, and both hands were plunged deep into her pockets. She held them together, wrapping the coat as tightly as she could against the wind. In her right hand, she clutched her tiny piece of home. The little red stone.

The dark sky was thick with heavy clouds, and the wind was fierce. It plucked at her with harsh fingers, whipping her hair about her face like ghostly seaweed in stormy currents.

Fear flooded her thoughts. Panic welled inside her like crashing waves. She shook her head and turned on the spot, wondering how she had got here without knowing it. One moment she had been asleep in bed, and now she was standing on the overgrown path.

'I'm not really here,' she told herself. 'I'm still in bed. Dreaming. It's the only thing that makes sense.'

But it was all so real. The wind. The cold earth beneath her feet.

The Weeping Tree.

Nisha looked at it standing on the crag.

'I'm still in bed,' she told herself again. 'I'm dreaming.'

It was the only explanation, and the more she said it, the more she believed it. The more she believed it, the calmer she became. And instead of fighting the dream, Nisha resigned herself to it. She allowed her fear to leave her like a heavy sigh as her thoughts settled and she wondered where the dream would take her.

'Nisha.'

And there he was, on the path ahead. Just a silhouette, but it was definitely him.

The boy.

'Come to the tree.'

He set off walking and Nisha followed without hesitation. She moved briskly, knowing that she was safe in her dream. But as she climbed towards the northern tip of the island, the boy slipped from view. One moment he was there, and then he wasn't. Nisha stopped and waited. She squinted into the darkness, wondering where he had gone, half expecting Mrs F to wake her for breakfast.

Just then, a gap appeared in the heavy clouds as if a hand had reached down from heaven to draw them aside like curtains. The crescent moon awoke in that perfect black. So clear and bright. It was as if a single eye was opening in the sky to watch her, and its silver light fell on the waves that surged on the North Sea beyond the island. The most marvellous thing was that everything fell into place at once. For an instant, the sea was no longer a cruel beast of chaos and death. For an instant it was something of utter beauty.

From where Nisha was standing, she could see the Weeping Tree on the crag with the tree house gripped in its claw. She had a perfect view of the moonlight playing on the waves beyond. Every time a wave crested and fell, glittering in the light, it gave the impression that the crooked tree was crying from the tips of its downturned branches.

The tree was weeping silver tears.

Extract from Nisha Barrow's Truth, 1942

As we drove away from the plantation, the sky got dark and a horrible smell came in through the car window. I knew it was burning rubber because it was the same as the smell at the kedai that time a pile of tyres got burnt, but this was much worse. There was black smoke coming out of the trees in the distance, getting thicker and blacker as if the whole world was going to end.

Papa said the workers were burning the factory so the Japanese couldn't use it. He said they were going to do the same with all the houses and I can't bear the thought of our bungalow all burnt up. All my clothes and toys and the trees and the flowers all gone.

Amma said Dewi and Seti were going back to their village because it wasn't safe for them on the plantation any more and that they'd get into trouble if the Japanese knew they had worked for us. I asked if it was bad to work for us.

'Of course not,' Amma said. 'Dewi and Seti are part of the family.' But that was even more confusing because if they are part of the family why couldn't they come to England with us? And I still didn't understand why the Japanese would punish them for working for us but Amma said, 'It's complicated,' which is one of the things grown-ups say when they don't want to explain something or tell the truth. Grown-ups always tell children that it's important to tell the truth ('honesty is the best policy' is what Papa always says) but I'm beginning to think grown-ups often don't tell the truth. I think they have all sorts of ways to keep secrets.

21

TWIG

A great sense of calm and comfort held her as she stood on the overgrown path. As she watched the tree weeping silver tears, the wind fell away to nothing but a gentle breeze, and she wanted only to be by that tree. It didn't draw her to it against her will; she went because she wanted to.

It was *all* she wanted.

She had forgotten about the boy. She had forgotten to care whether she was dreaming or awake. She didn't feel the sharpness of the rocky ground on her bare feet. She didn't feel the scratch of the thorns on her ankles and shins.

Spellbound, she walked on until she reached the end of the path where the Weeping Tree stood in its own small clearing at the edge of the cliff. It was as if nothing would grow around it. Or as if nothing was *allowed* to grow around it.

Nisha sat cross-legged on the stony earth beneath the branches. She felt that part of her wasn't inside her own body, but flying high above it, looking down at herself. A lonely girl beneath a lonely tree.

With that thought, she remembered Amma lying ill in bed and she wished more than anything that she would be well again. She wished that Papa had escaped the terror of Singapore, and that he was safe and well and on his way home. She wished her grandmother's icy heart would melt. She wished—

'Don't be afraid.'

Nisha looked up with a start.

The boy had stepped from behind the tree.

'Don't be afraid,' he said again.

Nisha couldn't see his face. He was close to the trunk of the tree, almost a part of it, standing in the shadow away from the moon's silver gaze.

'Who are you?' Nisha asked.

'My name is Twig.' His voice was gentle and calming. A whisper of wind. She heard it as if he had spoken right into her mind.

'Where are you from?' she asked. 'Do you live on the

island?'

'In a way.'

'Are you a ghost?'

Twig didn't move. 'I am the heart of the Weeping Tree.'

'What does that mean?'

'It means different things to different people.'

Nisha frowned. 'That doesn't make sense.'

'Things don't always have to make sense. Does it make sense that you're here right now, under the tree with me?'

Nisha shook her head. 'No. I suppose not.'

'But you're wondering if you're dreaming or awake.'

'Yes.'

'Does it matter?' Twig came forward. 'Either way, I'm right here.'

Nisha didn't make any attempt to move when Twig sat down in the shadows beside her. He was close enough that she could feel the cold surrounding him, but she didn't feel afraid, though she didn't understand why.

'You're not afraid of me because I don't want to hurt you,' Twig said as if he had plucked the thought from Nisha's head. 'I want to help you.'

'Why?'

Twig frowned. 'Because you *need* my help.'

Nisha took a deep breath and watched the waves flickering silver. Even the sea looked calm now. As if it were black treacle, moving in slow motion.

'How do you know what I'm thinking?' Nisha asked. 'Can you read my mind?'

'Sometimes.'

'I've seen you before,' Nisha said. 'Haven't I? Three times. I saw you when I first came here. Then in the storm. And again, in the garden.'

'I've been calling you.'

'Can anyone else see you?' It suddenly excited Nisha that she might be the only one who could see Twig. Her own special friend.

'I come to those who need me, but they don't always want to see.'

'Need you? What do you mean?'

Twig gently pulled Nisha's hand from her pocket. His touch was cold as he carefully opened her fingers, and Nisha knew she had felt it before.

Twig took the stone from Nisha's open palm and held it up to the moonlight to inspect it.

'You're sad,' he said. 'And you're losing hope. I can feel it all around you.'

Nisha didn't say anything.

'But you must have hope.'

'I'm trying,' she said. 'I know Amma will get better and that Papa will be here soon. I just . . .' She felt tears in her eyes. They welled in her lower lids and spilt down her cheeks. 'Everything feels so hopeless but I really want to believe things will get better. I really do.'

'Then, believe.' Twig lowered the hand holding the red stone and reached out with the other one to wipe away Nisha's tears. 'Is it really so hard?'

'Yes.'

'I can help you,' Twig said. 'I can watch over your amma and your papa. Make them safe.'

'How?' Nisha sniffed.

They were close now, just inches apart, but shadows fell across Twig's delicate features so that Nisha couldn't quite see him. His face was somehow vague and beyond seeing. It was as if the night were trying to hide him from her.

His eyes glinted silver when he put the stone back on the palm of Nisha's hand and closed her fingers around it.

'How?' Nisha asked again. 'How can you help me? How can you make Amma and Papa safe?'

Twig turned and looked out to sea. 'I am the heart of the tree.' He said it as if it explained everything that could ever need explaining.

'But what can you do?' Nisha asked. 'What can you *actually* do?'

'I can help them if you agree to do something for me.' Twig looked at her again and Nisha was lost in his eyes. Suddenly it didn't matter how or why. All that mattered was Amma and Papa.

Nisha squeezed the stone and sat up straight. 'I'll do anything.' As soon as she said it, a shadow of doubt crossed her mind. Would she *really* do anything? What if it was something dangerous? What if Twig asked her to jump off the cliff into the sea?

'I won't ask you to do that,' he said. 'I would never ask you to do that.'

Nisha took a deep breath of still air. 'What then? What do I have to do?'

'You have to find three lost treasures and bring them to me here under the Weeping Tree. When the full moon is gold.'

'Gold?'

'You'll see.'

'What three treasures?'

'That's the difficult part,' he said. 'I can't tell you.'

'You can't tell me?' Nisha felt her heart grow heavy. 'But how can I find something if I don't even know what I have to find?'

'You'll know when you find them.' Twig put a cold hand over Nisha's heart. 'You'll know it here.'

'But how do I look for them?'

'I can't answer that,' he said. 'I can't tell you how or what or where.'

'That's mean.' Nisha's shoulders slumped as she turned to watch the waves. 'How could I ever find something if I don't know what to look for?'

'Don't give up now,' Twig said. 'Don't give up before you have even begun. You must have hope. And courage.'

Nisha closed her eyes. Hope. It was such an easy word to say but not such an easy thing to feel when she was so far from home and so many terrible things had happened.

'Why can't you just help them?' she asked. 'Why do I have to find three lost treasures?'

'It's the way,' Twig said. 'Don't you even want to try?'

'Of course. If you can help Amma and Papa, I'll do anything.'

'Good. But there are rules.'

'Rules?' Nisha looked into Twig's silvery eyes. 'There are already so many rules here.'

'And I have three more. First, you must wear this around your wrist.' Twig held up what looked like a bracelet made from the blackest wood. 'And you must never lose it.'

Nisha said nothing.

'Second, you must find all three treasures and return to me here before the full moon turns from gold to silver.'

Nisha waited for the third rule.

'The third rule is the hardest of all,' Twig said. 'You must not tell anyone about this. Not about me, nor about our agreement. Don't even mention my name. Do you understand?'

'I think so.'

'You have to *know* so.'

'Yes. All right. I understand.'

'Then put this on and the agreement is made.' Twig

held out the bracelet. 'In return for three lost treasures, I will help your amma and papa.'

Before she knew what she was doing, Nisha put the stone into her pocket, then reached forward and slipped her right hand through the bracelet.

It was the strangest thing. As soon as she put her fingers through it, she felt an icy chill burn through her skin. It was like thrusting her hand into the cold sea. There was even a curious resistance, as if the air inside the bracelet was thicker than the air outside it. As if she were pushing through a fine barrier of water. But once her hand was all the way through and Twig let go of the bracelet, it tightened, drawing close to her wrist, clinging to her like a living vine.

A wave of exhaustion swept over her. It rose from the bracelet, growing up her arm and spreading out to engulf her. Nisha's eyelids became heavy as she looked first at Twig, then out at the silver-tipped waves of the cold North Sea.

As she watched, the clouds above began to shift. They drifted close together, drawing across the crescent moon until the crag was in darkness once more.

When Nisha looked back at the tree, Twig was gone. Before she could call his name, exhaustion overcame her and sleep carried her away.

SEVEN DAYS UNTIL FULL MOON

22
GHOSTS

Nisha awoke feeling confused. She had been on the crag just a few moments ago, but now she was tucked up in bed in Barrow House.

The blackout curtains were still drawn across the window, but enough morning daylight leaked in to show the room in a murky grey light. At the end of the bed was a large wooden chest – Nisha knew it was full of bed linen because she and Joy had checked before she went to sleep last night. There was the desk and chair beneath the window, the washstand in the corner, and the small table by the bed. Beside it was a comfortable chair with Nisha's clothes draped over it, ready for her to wear.

Nisha was not on the crag. She was not beneath the Weeping Tree.

It had all been a dream.

She rubbed her eyes with both hands, wondering if she could face another day on Barrow Island, and that's when she felt it on her wrist.

The bracelet.

She pulled her hands away from her face, expecting it to be her imagination, but there it was, around her right wrist. The wooden bracelet.

Nisha stared at it.

It didn't make sense. She had no memory of walking to the crag or of getting back. But the bracelet meant that she must have been there. Unless it had made its way on to her wrist some other way. Could someone have come into the room in the night and put it there?

Nisha touched it with her fingertips, as if it might bite her. It felt unnaturally cold. She gripped it and tried to remove it, but it was too narrow to slip over the wide part of her hand.

She threw back the covers and went to the window, thinking she would need better light to inspect the bracelet. There had to be a fastening somewhere – a way to take it off. But as she crossed the room, she felt grit between her toes, and when she opened the curtains and looked down, she was shocked to see her dirty feet on the bare floorboards. They were caked in dry mud, and the

hem of her nightdress was filthy, as if it had trailed
through long, wet grass. Her feet and ankles were covered
in fine cuts and scratches.

Confused, Nisha turned around and saw dirty footprints leading from the door to the threadbare rug at the
side of the bed. And when she returned to the bed and
pulled the covers all the way back, she found mud and
grass on the sheets.

Still in her nightdress, Nisha dropped into the armchair
beside her bed and stared at the footprints on the rug.
The only explanation was that she had been outside.

So, maybe it *was* real. Or, at least, she had *definitely*
been sleepwalking.

She looked down at her hands resting on her knees,
almost afraid to see the bracelet around her wrist. But
there it was.

Still there.

It was wooden, as she remembered it from last night.
And when she turned it around her wrist, she saw three
scratched marks where something might be written. But
the marks were blurred, as if Nisha was looking at them
through tears. The strangest thing was that although her
skin was warm, the bracelet felt cold. Dead. But it didn't
make her uneasy to have it on her wrist. If anything, it
made her feel calm.

And if the bracelet was real, then Twig must be real.

And if Twig was real, then maybe her agreement with him was also real. She didn't have to understand it, she just had to know that it was so. She didn't know how birds could fly or trees could blossom or how the earth turned, but all those things still happened. They were a kind of magic all of their own.

As Nisha brushed away the dry mud and got dressed, many confused thoughts fell over themselves in her head. But most of all she wondered what three treasures she had to find, and where she would find them.

As soon as Nisha was ready, she went to check on Amma.

Joy was sitting in the armchair, a cup of tea beside her on the small, round table.

'Is she any better?' Nisha went to sit on the edge of the bed. She ran a hand over Amma's forehead.

Amma managed little more than to open her eyes just a crack, and only for a moment. She made a noise deep in her throat.

'Just the same.' Joy looked tired.

But Nisha thought Amma looked worse than yesterday. Her breathing was shallow, and the colour was faded from her skin. She looked as if she might be dying, and Nisha decided right there and then that she would do whatever she could to find those three treasures for Twig.

If it was real.

'Did you look in on me last night?' Nisha asked.

'I did.' Joy stood up and stretched. 'You were sleeping like a log.'

'I didn't get up? Or move?'

'Definitely not. I checked a few times and you were fast asleep – which is what *I* need to be right now. It's time for me to go,' she yawned. 'I'll get a few hours' sleep before I'm on rat-catching duty again.' She lifted both arms and pretended to aim along the barrel of a shotgun.

Nisha put her left hand over the shape of the bracelet hidden inside her sleeve. 'Joy?'

'Aye, what is it?'

'Do you believe in ghosts?'

'Ghosts?' Joy stopped what she was doing and gave Nisha a serious look. 'Why do you ask?'

Nisha shrugged. 'It's just—' Twig had said that she couldn't tell anyone. Not a soul. 'I suppose . . . because this place is so creepy.'

Joy lowered her voice as if she were confiding in Nisha. 'I agree. There are some strange noises in the night. But it's just the house settling. Buildings do that, you know, especially old ones like this.'

Nisha nodded.

'There's the sea, too,' Joy said. 'And the wind sometimes sounds as if . . .' She stopped and looked out of the window as if she were trying to remember something important. 'I should be off.' She shook herself – *actually shook herself* – then picked up her book and retrieved her coat that was on a hanger hooked over the edge of the wardrobe. 'I'll see you soon. We'll dance again, you and I.' Joy wiggled her eyebrows then put out her hands as if she were holding a partner, and danced across to the door.

'Wait.' Nisha stopped her. 'What were you going to say about the wind? What does it sound like?'

Joy stood with one hand on the doorknob, the door half open. She frowned as she looked back at Nisha. 'Things play tricks on you at night,' she said. 'You know that, right?'

Nisha nodded.

'Well, there were times last night when it sounded as if . . . as if the wind was calling my name.' She smiled and shrugged. 'Silly, I know, but there it is.'

23
GRANDMOTHER

As Nisha neared the bottom of the stairs, Mrs Barrow appeared from her study like a wraith.

Humphrey, the little coarse-haired terrier, trotted past her and came to greet Nisha with a snort. His whole body wriggled with the force of his wagging tail. When he jumped up and put his paws on Nisha's legs, she rubbed his head and patted his belly.

'Humphrey!' Mrs Barrow snapped her fingers.

The dog stopped and looked at her expectantly.

'Kitchen.'

With a clickety-click of nails on stone, he skidded out of the hallway and along the passage towards the kitchen.

He barked once, then came the creak of rusty hinges and Mrs F's voice as she let him in.

Mrs Barrow remained by the study door and spoke across the hallway at Nisha: 'I can't have you moping around the house all day like a wet weekend.'

Nisha felt so small standing at the bottom of the enormous staircase.

'I've told Mrs Foster that I want you to earn your keep. I instructed her to put you to work darning socks and so on, but she insisted that you need fresh air and exercise.' Mrs Barrow put her hands behind her back and took a deep breath. 'Now, I don't believe it's dignified for a young lady to be running wild outside like an animal, but I concur with her observations that you are a rather sickly-looking child. I have agreed that you can go to the mainland today and collect a few things from the village. Mrs Foster will give you a list. She will also furnish you with all the relevant coupons.'

'I was going to stay with Am—' Nisha remembered what Mrs F had told her yesterday. 'With *Mother*.'

'Well, yes, I'm sure you're concerned for her well-being – as are we all.'

Nisha didn't believe that for a second.

'But Mrs Foster is taking good care of her, and I'm already paying for a land girl to help, so there's no sense in you spending all day in that room feeling sorry for yourself. And you *do* look rather sickly, as I say, so perhaps

Mrs Foster is right – perhaps fresh air *is* the right thing for you. But I can't have you running willy-nilly around the island. Do I make myself clear?'

Nisha understood exactly what Mrs Barrow was getting at. She was talking about the garden. Nisha wished she hadn't said anything about it. She would have liked to go there again, but now it felt like it was out of bounds along with everything else.

'I'm sorry I upset you yesterday,' Nisha said.

'Never mind that. What's done is done. I've asked Mrs Foster to find a bicycle for you. Are you able to ride a bicycle? I assume they have such things in Malaya?'

Nisha nodded.

'Well, you can ride to the mainland and collect the shopping.' Mrs Barrow gave her a long stern look, then something softened in her expression. 'I know I can be strict,' she said. 'But it's never without good reason. I accept your apology. Thank you. It was given like a lady, and . . . I'm sorry I snapped at you yesterday. You may use the flower garden if you wish. It's a comforting place. A good place to collect your thoughts. But take care of it. Don't stand in the beds, and don't touch the flowers. And you must never,' she held up a finger, '*never*, be tempted to go to the Keep or to the tree, do you understand? Stay away from the tree.'

'Yes. Thank you, Gra— *Mrs Barrow.*'

'Very well.' Mrs Barrow lowered her hand. 'And . . .'

She sighed and stared down at the floor before looking at Nisha once again. 'And if you would like to call me "Grandmother", that would be acceptable.'

24

A BIT OF LIFE AND COLOUR

Mr Foster had cleaned off an old bicycle so it was ready for Nisha to use. He was working in the courtyard at the back of the house, just outside the scullery door, putting a drop of oil on the chain.

In one of the stables on the other side of the square, a couple of other bikes were leaning against the wall beside the trap they'd used to travel to Barrow Island from the train station. There was also a car-shaped bulge hidden by a huge green tarpaulin.

'Petrol's rationed,' Mr Foster said when he saw Nisha looking. 'Bonny's our transport now.'

Bonny was in her own stable next to the stone

archway, with her head poking out into the cold. All the other stables were empty. Nisha counted eight in total, and thought that Barrow House must have once been very grand.

Humphrey was sitting by the entrance to the courtyard, watching three chickens scratching at the straw-covered stones. When he saw Nisha come down the steps, he ran over, tail wagging.

Nisha's grandmother wasn't there to call him away, so she sat on the bottom step and let him jump up at her.

Voices on *Kitchen Front* wafted out from the wireless in the kitchen while Nisha stroked Humphrey's head and patted his side. When he started licking her face, she pushed him away and went to see Bonny instead. Bonny nodded in approval as Nisha rubbed her neck and breathed in the warm smell of hay and manure and horse sweat.

It was a surprisingly good smell.

'I've cleaned 'er up,' Mr Foster said. 'Should ride like she's new.'

Nisha thought he was talking about Bonny until she turned around to see him stretch his back and push up his cap to admire the bicycle.

The freshly wiped black paint caught the light and gleamed.

'It's beautiful.' Nisha came closer to inspect it.

'Aye, she's a beauty all reet. BSA All-Weather Bicycle,'

Mr Foster said. 'Built to last. Men rode these into battle in the Great War.'

'The Japanese soldiers rode bicycles through the jungle,' Nisha said.

'What's that?'

'Nothing.' She buried the thought and locked it away, turning her attention back to the bicycle.

Thin gold trim threaded around the mudguards and along the frame. At the very front, above the tyre, a trademark symbol of three crossed rifles announced the manufacturer – the Birmingham Small Arms Company.

'I remember seeing your fatha racin' down to the village on this,' Mr Foster said.

Nisha took the bicycle by the handlebars.

'This was Papa's?' she asked.

'Aye, the very same one. He must've been about your age when he got it. It'll be a treat to see you ridin' it down to the village like he did.'

Nisha squeezed the handlebars and wondered where Papa was right now.

'Mind you watch the tide, though,' Mr Foster said. 'Divvent get caught on the causeway when it's comin' in. If it looks unsafe, then it is. That water comes in fast.'

'Is it all right to cross now?' Nisha asked.

'It'll be good for a few hours now. Best be back across by one, though, else you'll be stuck on the mainland.'

'Divvent forget these.' Mrs F stepped down from the scullery with a list and a handful of folded coupons. She came over to Nisha and pressed them into her hand. 'Straight across the causeway and into the village,' she said. 'You can't miss it.'

Nisha tucked everything into her pocket then swung her leg over the bicycle and settled on the chestnut-leather seat. She set the pedals to the right position, but as she was about to set off, Mrs F handed her a knitted bag and leant close enough for Nisha to smell the carbolic soap on her.

'Mrs Barrow's been asking about your mam,' she said. 'Visited her a couple of times yesterday, and once this morning. She'd never say it, or act like it, but I reckon somewhere deep down she's pleased to have you bring a bit of life and colour to this dreary old island.'

Nisha looked at Mrs F in surprise, but before she could say anything, Mrs Foster gave her a wink and retreated back into the warmth of the scullery.

Nisha wobbled a little as she crossed the courtyard and headed through the archway to join the drive. It was difficult to ride on the gravel, and the bike was bigger than she was used to, but she soon got the hang of it. And once she was on the road, she pedalled hard as if she were in Malaya riding back from the club after dark. The harder she pedalled, the brighter the dynamo would burn.

White light would flood on to the road and she would chase it home, where Dewi would cook spicy noodles for supper and put Nisha to bed between cool cotton sheets. Later Amma and Papa would drive back in the car and Nisha would pretend to be asleep when they came in to kiss her goodnight.

Back on Barrow Island, the cold wind blew those thoughts from Nisha's head, but it was wonderful to feel the breeze on her face. The movement and exercise were liberating. She felt lighter too, because Mrs Barrow had asked her to call her 'Grandmother'. It made Nisha feel more welcome in the house – even more so after what Mrs F had just told her about Grandmother visiting Amma and being pleased to have some more life on the island.

Humphrey ran alongside her for a while but soon became overexcited. He started yapping and running in front of the bike to bite the tyre. He was making all sorts of noises, growling and trying to sound fierce, and Nisha couldn't help laughing.

It didn't last long, though, because an image came to her of Amma lying feverish in bed. It didn't seem right that Nisha should be enjoying herself. She suddenly felt guilty that she was laughing, and that made her think of David Hill and all that business that had happened on the convoy from the plantation down to Singapore.

And when Nisha reached the causeway, she remembered Mr Foster's warning.

That water comes in fast.

She stopped on the dunes and looked at the stone path snaking across the vast stretch of flat sand between Barrow Island and the mainland. Halfway, the refuge hut stood tall on its narrow stilts like a strange bird waiting for the water to come in. She didn't *ever* want to need it, and reminded herself that the sea was far behind her now, so it should be fine. Mr Foster had said it would be safe for a few hours.

Humphrey whined impatiently, but Nisha ignored him and looked back. The Keep was out of sight now, as was the Weeping Tree, but she could see the house standing lonely at the centre of the island. Such a grey place, she thought, but perhaps it *had* gained a little colour. The dull, washed-out ivy looked greener than she remembered it. And, for the first time, she noticed that the front door, half hidden beneath the outer porch, was painted red.

As Nisha watched, the door opened and her grandmother emerged from the house. She stood for a moment, then turned and took the path towards the walled garden.

She wasn't alone.

The skinny boy followed a few paces behind her.

Twig.

But Grandmother took no notice of him. Only once did she pause and look back. She stood and stared, as if she were looking right at Twig, but then shook her head and continued along the path as if she hadn't seen him. When she disappeared from view, the boy stopped and turned in Nisha's direction. The wind picked up and blew across the island towards her. It brought the scent of the sea and she heard her name whispered in its breath.

She shivered and thought about their meeting beneath the Weeping Tree. Their agreement. Three treasures she had to find, but what were they? How would she ever know?

She pushed up her sleeve and looked at the bracelet around her wrist. She studied the three scratched and blurry markings, wondering if they were a clue.

Far away, over the sea, a solitary gull cried to the waves, and when Nisha looked up at the house again the boy had vanished.

Extract from Nisha Barrow's Truth, 1942

It took ages to get to Singapore. Really, it was probably just a few days, but it felt like weeks. There were lots of other people going there and Papa said we were travelling in a 'convoy'. Every day more people joined, all travelling in their own little groups but part of this long line of cars snaking through the plantations and patches of jungle.

Sometimes we saw army trucks and soldiers going in different directions. There was always a bit of fuss when it happened because everyone would try to get some news about how close the Japanese were. It always felt like they were right behind us. One day, a truck full of wounded soldiers went past, and all the men in our convoy took off their hats.

Christmas Day came and went and no one said much about it. I suppose no one felt like celebrating anything so we just kept on driving.

Every day we drove until it started to get dark, then we pulled over at the side of the road with the rest of the convoy. Usually people who knew each other kept together in little groups, keeping their cars close. If we were near a village, Malays would come to look because they had never seen white people before. The children would just stare, sometimes coming right up to the car windows to look inside. Other times people came on bicycles loaded up with things to sell – fruit and sweets and cans of petrol and chickens with their feet tied.

In the morning, we would drive away again, trying to keep ahead of the Japanese.

'They're catching up,' people would say. 'We need to keep going.'

One time when we stopped there was a water buffalo pulling a wooden wagon loaded with papayas and rambutans and bananas. I wish they had proper fruit here in England, but there's just bland food and not much of it.

Anyway, the time with the water buffalo cart, we stopped for the night and got out to stretch our legs. As usual, all the grown-ups stood in a group whispering so the children couldn't hear what they were saying. Amma bought me a bag of rambutans, so I went away from everyone and sat on my own at the edge of the road and stared into the jungle.

It's amazing what you can see in there if you just watch. All kinds of birds. Little flashes of colour. There are insects on the leaves if you look carefully, and at night there are fireflies that flicker like stars in the sky. Or tiny golden teardrops. Dewi once told me they're the fingernails of ghosts passing in the jungle but I think she just said that to stop me from going out after dark. There are sounds in there too, whistles and calls and the quietest rustling, but most of all I like the smell that you don't get anywhere else. It's warm and damp and full of life. It's fresh and rotten at the same time and smells best right after the rain.

For a little while I watched the trees and forgot about the Japanese and the bombs and Seti and Dewi getting left behind. Instead I just listened to the evening, but then David Hill came over and stood right in front of me and said something like, 'Exciting, isn't it?' which it wasn't, it was scary and sad and horrible, so I told him that. David Hill was one of those on-and-off friends who was sometimes all right and sometimes not – like when he was at school with all his other friends and he was trying to show off (so annoying!). That's when he said stupid things. He probably didn't mean them, but when he said, 'You don't even need to evacuate. You and your mother are brown enough to go and live in the village with the natives and no one would know the difference. The Japanese would leave you alone,' it made my blood boil. Especially the way he said 'natives' as if Dewi and Seti aren't important. He probably thought he was being funny, but there was nothing funny about it. He once said Papa might as well have married a servant because Amma has brown skin like the Malays, but Amma isn't Malay, she's Indian, which makes me half Indian, which I like, and anyway, what's wrong with being Malay? I love Seti and Dewi, and most of the Malay people I know are a hundred times nicer than David Hill.

I stood up and told him he wasn't funny and that he didn't have to be an idiot all the time. Then I said that the only good thing about leaving the plantation was that I wouldn't have to look at his stupid face at school every day, so he called me a name I don't want to even write here because it's ghastly. After that, I said something I didn't mean. I wish I hadn't.

I wish I could take it back, but it's too late now

25

ON THE MAINLAND

Leaving Humphrey behind, Nisha raced along the causeway. She was terrified that the sea would come in and surround her. As if it were not controlled by the earth and the moon but that it was a living thing; watching her, waiting for another chance to claim her.

Down and down into the dark.

She expelled the thought and concentrated on the stone path and rode as fast as she could. A couple of times, her tyres skidded on seaweed lying on the road, but she stayed on track. She hardly even glanced up at the refuge hut as she passed it.

It took longer than expected to cross – at least ten

minutes – so when she finally left the causeway and rode up between the dunes towards the mainland, Nisha let out a sigh of relief. She came to a stop and looked back.

The air was clearer than it had been when she first saw Barrow Island, just two days ago. The misty fret was gone and the island was smaller than she remembered. At its heart, Barrow House sat brooding in dark isolation as if it were not quite of this world. There, too, was the broken Keep, and the Weeping Tree standing on the crag.

The sea was right out, exposing the wet sand where the huge concrete cubes stretched out in a line like thuggish sentries. In the distance were the red and blue smudges of fishing boats lying idle. Closer, a grey concrete pillbox hid in the grass on the highest dune, waiting patiently for an invasion. For a moment, Nisha thought she heard the rattle of machine gun fire, and the scream of planes diving from the sky to strafe bullets across the sand and—

She shook her head to get rid of those black thoughts. She wished they'd go away. She wished she could forget all about them.

The heart of Morbury was a single potholed road with a short parade of shops on one side and a village green on the other. A few children were playing football on the grass, their shouts punctuated by the hollow thump of boots kicking leather. Beyond them, a confused collection of cottages stretched back towards the fields. In the distance, crows circled in the grey sky.

Nisha came to a stop by the shops and looked at the signage over each one. Hartley's Butchery. Smaile's Hardware. Smith & Son Fruiterer. F.W. Carr Groceries.

A group of young women wandered past, laughing and talking. They wore a uniform of green jumpers and brown breeches, and several of them had their hair cut short, like Joy's. Nisha found herself wondering if these were land girls, but was disappointed not to see Joy's friendly face among them. They fell silent and watched Nisha with interest as they passed, suddenly making her feel very self-conscious. She remembered how the people of Morbury had stared when she and Amma first arrived. Once again she had the impression that everyone was watching her. She glanced over her shoulder to see that the children had stopped playing and were looking in her direction. A group of women standing by the bright red postbox on the opposite side of the road was casting glances her way as they spoke in quiet voices.

Nisha put her hand into her pocket and touched the red stone for reassurance.

She left her bike lying on the pavement and pushed into the grocery shop. It was empty except for the man behind the counter. Wearing a brown overcoat and a flat cap, he was reading a newspaper laid out in front of him. But when the bell tinkled over the door, he took off his glasses and looked up.

Nisha stayed where she was, and the two of them watched each other for a few moments before the man said, 'You're Mrs Barrow's granddaughter.'

Nisha nodded and let her eyes shift, taking in the display of tins and jars and packets that lined the shelves. She was especially drawn to the large jars of sweets right behind the shopkeeper.

She had never seen a shop quite like it. At home in Malaya the shops were open-fronted, with smelly drains running along the outside. They were a marvellous jumble of spice baskets, bright pink sweets, and huge tins of pastes. Delicious fruits hung from twine or were arranged in great colourful piles. Sacks of rice were stacked like mountains, and there was the smell of cloves and dirt and spoilt fruit and cooking all mixed up in one wonderful wall of perfume.

Here, everything was arranged into neat and boring rows on the shelves. Everything smelt of wood and cardboard and fresh vegetables still dirty from the field.

'Do you have a name?' he asked.

She nodded.

'Is it a secret?'

She shook her head and cleared her throat. 'Nisha.'

'Nisha? That's a bonny name. Nisha.' He tested the sound of it a few more times then spread his arms wide.

'Well, I'm Mr Carr. Welcome to my shop.' He leant forward on the counter. 'What can I get for you, Nisha?'

'I . . . have a list.' Nisha held up the piece of paper.

'From Mrs Foster? Excellent. Mrs Foster writes an excellent list. And you have all the coupons?' Mr Carr held out his hand.

Nisha bundled everything together and gave it to him.

Mr Carr put on his glasses. 'Mm-hm. Aye. Aye. Excellent. Uh-huh. Eee-xcellent.' He muttered to himself as he read through the list, tracking each item with a finger. 'I think we have all that. It'll take us a minute or two to put it together, so in the meantime . . .' He took a large jar from the shelf behind him and unscrewed the lid before holding it out to Nisha. 'Sherbet lemon? It's on me, but divvent tell anyone or I'll get into bother.' He tapped the side of his nose. '"There's a war on" an' all that carry-on.'

Nisha hesitated, but the delightfully sweet smell of sticky lemons made her mouth water. It was a long time since she'd had anything properly sweet.

'Go on,' he urged.

She carefully put her hand into the jar and took one of the hard, yellow sweets.

Mr Carr mimed putting it into his mouth, so Nisha did as he suggested and immediately felt an explosion of taste. It was exactly like lemon, but even better.

'Good, eh?' Mr Carr smiled. 'Those are my favourite.'

Nisha nodded. 'Thank you.'

'My pleasure.' He took two sweets from each jar on the shelf and put them in a paper bag which he twirled at the corners and handed to Nisha. 'Pop them in your pocket,' he said with a wink. 'For when you need a treat. It'll be our secret.'

Nisha didn't know how to thank him. His kindness, and the thought of having all that flavour in her pocket, brought a lump to her throat and tears to her eyes. But Mr Carr just held up his hand and shook his head.

'Say nothin',' he told her. 'I'll get your order together.'

When he turned away, picking tins and packets from the shelf and putting them into Nisha's knitted bag, the bell tinkled over the door, and the gaggle of women who had been standing outside bustled in. They brought with them a wave of sea air that smothered the comforting smell of the shop.

'I'll be with you in a tick, ladies,' Mr Carr called over his shoulder.

The women stood gossiping in whispers by the door.

'. . . Charles Barrow's bairn . . . Malaya or some such place . . . shoulda married a proper English girl . . .'

Nisha tried not to hear what they were saying, but their voices grew louder the more excited they became.

'. . . dark skin . . . I mean, who do they think they are? . . . foreigners . . .'

'. . . refugees . . .'

Nisha couldn't help glancing over her shoulder, but immediately wished she hadn't.

There were three of them huddled together looking directly at her. When Nisha turned around, they stopped talking but didn't have the decency to look away. They glared at her, actually *glared* at her as if she shouldn't have been there, and Nisha wanted to run out of the shop there and then. She had to be firm with herself to stay and wait for Mr Carr to finish. He had been so kind to her, it wouldn't be right for her to run out on him.

'Ladies.' Mr Carr's voice edged into Nisha's thoughts. 'Be kind.'

The women harrumphed and looked offended at his comment.

'Here you are.' Mr Carr handed Nisha the shopping bag. 'I've put everythin' in there. Mind how you gan.'

'Thank you.' Nisha took the bag and pushed past the women. She was desperate to escape the shop as quickly as she could.

'How rude!'

'No manners!'

'Foreigners!'

Nisha kept her eyes down as she left. She didn't want to see anyone. She just wanted to get back to the island and to be with Amma, so she hurried to her bicycle and hung the bag over the handlebars. Turning the bicycle around, she jumped on and quickly pedalled out on to the road.

'Oi!'

Nisha glanced up to see a boy standing right in front of her. For a fraction of a second, she thought it was Twig, and she gasped, causing a searing pain in her chest as the sherbet lemon sucked down inside her. At the same time, she jerked the handlebars and braked, but she was already moving too fast to avoid the boy. Before she could make sense of what was happening, she hit him full-on. She knocked him down and sent him skidding backwards like a rag doll. Then the tyres slipped away from beneath her, and the bike toppled over with a jarring crash.

But that wasn't the worst of it. Not by a long way.

26

GYPSY BLOOD

The sherbet lemon was lodged like a stone in Nisha's chest. She tried to take a breath, but nothing happened. She tried to breathe out, but nothing. She tried to swallow, to push the sweet down, but her throat only tightened.

She couldn't breathe.

Immediately, she began to panic. It was an awful feeling of drowning. She had felt it before, in the docks at Singapore, and visions of that awful day came flooding back. Suddenly she was there again, lungs burning with salt water. The screams and the fire and the awful drag of the sea.

Down and down into the dark.

'Why divvent you bloody watch where you're gannin'?' A scruffy-looking boy was sitting on the other side of the crashed bike. He was picking grit out of the grazes on his skinny knees and flicking it away in disgust.

He scowled at her as he got to his feet. 'Stupid lass, look at this!' He plucked at the hole in the elbow of his jumper. 'Me mam's gonna kill us. She'll bray us with a belt and make us mend this before I can have any tea.'

Nisha's eyes began to bulge. She put her hands to her throat as if she might be able to claw it open and pull out the sherbet lemon. She didn't want to die, but that's what was going to happen if she couldn't get it out of her chest.

'I should give you a thick ear.' The boy curled his hands into fists, but when he looked at Nisha, seeing her properly for the first time, he stopped dead. 'What's the matter wi' ya?'

Nisha gripped her throat and opened her mouth. Her whole chest was burning and she wanted to tell the boy that she was choking, that she was going to die, but no sound would come out of her.

The boy leapt into action. He ran around behind Nisha and pulled her up on to her knees. Then he bent her forward and hit her between the shoulder blades as hard as he could.

Once.

Twice.

Three times.

On the fourth strike, the sherbet lemon shot out of Nisha's mouth and skidded across the road.

Nisha gasped a huge breath, sucking the air deep inside her.

The boy scooted round to sit in front of her. 'Hell's bells, are you all reet?'

Nisha replied with a giant sob followed by a fit of coughing that made her ribs hurt. She was glad not to be choking any more, but her throat was on fire and tears were streaming down her cheeks. Her nose was running too.

'Let us help you up,' the boy said. 'I'm sorry I shouted at you.'

But when he tried to help Nisha to her feet, she pushed him away. She was scared and embarrassed and wanted to be anywhere but here. Coughing and sobbing, she gathered up the spilt groceries and stuffed them back into the bag. What she then wanted to do most of all was jump on the bike and ride away. But to her dismay, the bike chain was hanging off, and that made her cry even more. Not only had she had knocked a boy over, and nearly choked to death, but now she had broken Papa's bike. Grandmother would be so cross she'd probably make Nisha call her 'Mrs Barrow' again. She felt awful. She wanted to disappear like a twist of sea fret snatched away by the wind.

By now the gossiping women had emerged from Mr Carr's shop to see what was going on. People stopped in the street or appeared from the other shops with a curious tinkling of bells. The children on the green stood watching, and the land girls peeped out from Smaile's Hardware shop. Even the old man in overalls in the garage at the far end of the street was standing with his hands on his hips, wondering what all the commotion was about.

'Let us help wi' that.' The boy reached for the bicycle, but Nisha turned and began wheeling it away along the road.

'Jamie Harper!' Mr Carr called from the door of his shop. 'You be a gentleman!'

'I am,' the boy said, throwing his hands in the air. 'I am!'

Nisha had thought Barrow Island was the worst place in the whole world, but now she knew better. The village of Morbury was *much* worse. She fixed her eyes on the road and marched away, wheeling the bike with both hands to keep it steady. Her chest was burning and her eyes and nose were streaming.

It wasn't long before she heard the thump-thump-thump of too-big boots on the road just behind her, and the huff-huff of heavy breathing.

'Didn't you hear us shoutin'?' the boy said as he caught up with her.

Nisha said nothing.

'Hey. You deaf or summat?'

'Yes.' She tapped her right ear. 'I am.'

'Oh. Em. Sorry.'

'Leave me be.' Nisha picked up her pace.

'That musta been a canny old fright.' The boy moved round to her left side and kept up with her. 'I know it was for *me*.'

He spoke with a thick accent and used words Nisha didn't always recognize. And his voice was quiet, so it was difficult to tell what he was saying. It was easier to just ignore him.

'Look, I'm sorry I shouted,' he said. 'I get like that sometimes. I divvent mean to, but ever since what happened to me fatha I have . . . Well, I have *moments*. That's what me mam says. I get angry, see, and I divvent knaa why.'

Nisha thought that if she took no notice of the angry, scruffy boy, then maybe he'd leave her alone.

'I *did* just save your life. The least you could do is say—'

'Thank you.' Nisha stopped and looked at him. 'Now will you please leave me al—'

'You're welcome.'

Nisha sighed and set off wheeling the bicycle again.

'I can mend your bike if you want.' The boy chased after her. 'It won't take us long.'

Nisha slowed down. Maybe it wasn't such a bad idea. If the boy could fix the bicycle, it would be better than her grandmother getting cross with her.

'Fine.' She stopped. 'But only if you show me how. In case it happens again.'

The boy looked impressed. 'Aye. Deal.' He spat on his hand and held it out to her.

'Ugh.' Nisha pulled a face.

The boy shrugged. 'If you divvent spit, it's not a deal.'

Nisha spat in the palm of her hand and grimaced as she shook with him. When he let go, she wiped her hand on the side of her coat.

'Hold the bike.' He crouched and grabbed the chain, leaving greasy marks all over his fingers. 'Watch. It's easy.'

It only took him a few seconds to put the chain over the gear, then he lifted the back wheel and spun the pedal with one hand. As if by magic, the chain looped itself around the gear and bit tight. 'All done.' He stood up and grinned.

'Thank you.'

'Nee botha. You headin' back to the island?' he asked. 'I'll walk with you if you like.'

Nisha didn't say anything, she just set off wheeling the bike along the road.

'I'm Jamie, by the way. What's your name?'

'Nisha.'

'Never heard that before. Is that from . . . wherever you come from?'

'Malaya,' Nisha said without looking at him.

'Ma-lay-a.' He tried the word a couple of times. 'Is it far away?'

'Yes.'

'I bet you miss it.'

Nisha really did. She missed it more than anything.

'Does everyone in Ma-lay-a have names like yours? Everyone here's called boring things like Jamie. Or Henry.'

'Actually, it's an Indian name. My amm— my *mother* is Indian.'

They weaved their way through the concrete road-block and headed out towards the sea where the sand dunes rose like a small mountain range.

'You're the talk of the village, ya knaa,' Jamie said. 'You and your mam. Nee one knows what to make of you.'

'Don't make anything of us,' Nisha told him. 'We're just people like everyone else.'

'Na, you're different. And I divvent mean because you look like you've got the best suntan ever. I mean . . .' He thought about it. 'Well, I divvent knaa what I mean. There's just summat about ya.'

Nisha wasn't sure if he was trying to compliment or insult her.

'But your fatha didn't come back did he? Is he still alive?'

'We don't know where he is.'

'That's horrible,' Jamie said. 'Maybe not knowing is worse than knowing. Mine got killed. He wasn't nothing fancy, like, just a soldier, but me mam says he did his duty. When I'm old enough I'll sign up and gan to fight the Germans for him.'

'How old are you?'

'Twelve.'

'Don't you want the war to be over by the time you're old enough?' Nisha asked.

'Maybe. Me mam says it's only a matter of time now the Americans are fightin' but . . .' Jamie shrugged. 'You never knaa.'

When they reached the dunes, Nisha stopped. She took the bag of sweets from her pocket and opened it to look inside. They smelt good, but the idea of eating them made her remember the panic of choking.

'You got sweets?' Jamie peered inside the bag with envy.

'D'you want them?' Nisha asked. 'I don't.' It seemed right to give them to him.

Jamie put his hands around the bag as if he were going to take it, but thought better of it. 'I'll have *one*,' he said. 'You keep the rest. You'll change your mind about 'em, you knaa. I once choked on a cola cube and me mam had to bang me on the back like I did for you. That's how I knew what to do.' He took a cola cube and put it in his mouth. 'You'll change your mind, I promise.'

'Just take them. Please.'

'Na. Keep 'em. But divvent eat 'em all. I'll have one next time I see you.'

Nisha stuffed the bag into her pocket, right on top of the red stone. She looked at her boots. 'Thank you. For saving my life.'

Jamie shrugged. 'Nee botha.' He turned to gaze out towards Barrow Island. 'I heard there's a tree over there that can make wishes come true.'

Nisha closed her eyes and took a deep breath.

'Me mam telt me it's called the Weepin' Tree. Is it true? Have you seen it?'

'I've seen it,' Nisha said. 'But I'm not allowed to go near it.'

'Can it really make wishes come true?'

Nisha shook her head. 'Nothing can make wishes come true.'

'That's not what me mam says, and she should knaa – she's a gypsy. I mean, not like a caravan gypsy, but she's got gypsy blood. I have too.'

Nisha thought about the tree. She tried to understand her strange sense of calm when she had been near it. It had felt like a dream, but the dirt on her feet had been real. The bracelet around her wrist was real.

'Will you show it me?' Jamie said.

'Hm?' Nisha's hand went to the bracelet hidden beneath her sleeve.

'The tree,' Jamie said. 'Will you show it me? Nee one's allowed on the island unless Mrs Foster says so, and most people are scared they'll get caught by the tide. But I'm not scared, and if I'm with you it'll be all reet so . . .'

'Maybe,' Nisha said. 'One day.'

'D'ya promise?'

Nisha didn't reply. She didn't want to make any promises she might have to break, so she climbed on to the bicycle, about to set off across the causeway. She put one foot on the pedals then looked at Jamie. 'I'm sorry about your father,' she said.

'Aye.' Jamie frowned. 'But we'll keep our fingers crossed for yours, eh?'

THREE DAYS UNTIL FULL MOON

27

NISHA BARROW'S TRUTH

Nisha didn't tell anyone about what happened in the
village. She spent the next few days helping
Mr Foster, digging and planting the vegetable garden, or
mending clothes and cooking with Mrs F in the kitchen.
And every evening she looked up to see the eye of the
moon opening wider behind the mask of clouds.

Amma's condition didn't improve at all. If anything,
it grew worse. Her temperature refused to come down,
and she hardly even moved when Nisha sat with her.
Doctor Michaels visited again to examine her, but he just
shook his head and said he was doing everything he
could.

'Best thing is to keep her comfortable,' he said. 'Keep her cool and make sure she gets some fluids, but that's all we can really do.' When he said it, he gave Nisha a sad look that she didn't quite understand.

If only she could find what Twig had told her to bring to the Weeping Tree. The three lost treasures. If she could do that, then everything would be all right. Amma would get better and Papa would be fine. She *had* to believe that. She had to believe that Twig could help, because there was nothing else left for her to believe in. But she couldn't make head nor tail of the strange markings on the bracelet, and she hadn't found anything that looked important. To make matters worse, Twig's words echoed in her mind.

'Before the full moon turns from gold to silver.'

Nisha had never seen a gold full moon, so she didn't know what that was, but she *did* know that the moon was growing bigger every day – and that meant time was running out.

'I wish everything was back to normal,' she said to Joy one evening.

They were in Amma's room, sitting on the floor playing Buccaneer. The game mat was unrolled between them, with the cards and tiny ships laid out on the squares. Joy had just boarded Nisha's ship and taken two barrels of rum and a gold bar.

'I think I've forgotten what that means,' Joy said.

'Normal. It seems like a very long time since I was home in Newcastle.'

'You must hate it here as much as I do,' Nisha said.

'Oh, I don't know.' Joy checked her cards then moved her ship to a new square. 'I don't *hate* it. I don't mind hard work, and it feels good to do my bit for the war.'

'But it's such a miserable place,' Nisha said. 'Everything's grey and cold.'

Joy laughed quietly. 'There's colour if you let yourself see it.'

'Is there?'

'Aye. Everywhere. Even on the island. What about all that beautiful yellow gorse?'

'Gorse?' Nisha asked. 'What's that?'

'Don't tell me you haven't seen them spiky bushes everywhere?' Joy said.

'Oh, that. It looks dull to me. Dull and grey.' But Nisha thought about the flowers in the secluded garden, and the red-tinged ivy climbing the walls of Barrow House.

Nisha took her turn to move her ship, but her heart wasn't really in it. She had too many other things on her mind.

'I was on the mainland the other day,' she said. 'There were some women talking about me and Amma, saying horrible things.'

'What sort of things?' Joy asked.

'Mean things about foreigners and refugees.'

'Silly old busybodies; just ignore them. You belong here as much as they do.'

'I don't belong here at all,' Nisha said. 'I belong in Malaya.' And suddenly her soul ached with longing to be barefoot in the sun. She wanted life and colour, and the sound of cicadas filling the world. She wanted to lie on her back in the grass beside Papa while they watched the fruit bats fly over at dusk. She wanted to hear the click of mahjong tiles from the veranda, and the gentle reassurance of Amma's soft voice.

'You belong wherever you want to belong,' Joy said, reaching across to brush the hair away from Nisha's face. 'Don't let anyone say otherwise.'

Nisha stood up and went to peer through a gap in the blackout curtains. 'The moon looks big,' she said. 'How long until it's full?'

'I don't know. Does it matter?'

Yes, it matters, Nisha thought. *It really, really matters*. 'No, I was just wondering.'

Joy came to join her at the window. 'Maybe a day or two left,' she said.

'And how long does it last?'

'Ah, well, I do know the answer to that because me brother's interested in these things. He said it actually only lasts an instant, even though it seems to last about three days.' Joy closed the curtains. 'But that's enough spooky stuff for one evening. Come over here and see what I brought for you.'

Joy reached behind the armchair and retrieved a brown paper bag. 'I wrapped it meself,' she said with a grin. 'Or I would have done if I'd had something to wrap it in. The brown bag will just have to do.'

Inside, Nisha found a notebook of lined paper, and a pencil. On the front of the notebook, written in neat handwriting, were the words 'Nisha Barrow's Truth'.

'It's . . .' Nisha flicked through the notebook of clean pages. 'Umm. Thank you.' It was a strange present.

'It's for you to write your story,' Joy said. 'Your own *truth*. Look.' She took the notebook and tapped the front cover. 'I wrote "Nisha Barrow's Truth" here so there's no mistake. You always look so thoughtful, as if something heavy is sitting on your shoulders, so I thought writing it down might help to make you feel lighter. Find somewhere quiet, and write everything down. Perhaps you could go to that flower garden you told me about. What have you got to lose?'

Extract from Nisha Barrow's Truth, 1942

I still remember what I said to David Hill that evening at the side of the road after he was rude to me. I said, 'I hope your house gets bombed.' I didn't mean it. I promise I didn't, but then he said, 'Well I hope _you_ get bombed,' and flicked me hard on my shoulder. I don't know why that made me so angry. Joy says we all try to put on a brave face, and Papa told me to be brave, so maybe that's what I was doing the whole time until David Hill flicked me on the shoulder. But after that I sort of broke and everything came flooding out. So I pushed him. He didn't fall over or anything, just stumbled a bit, then he shoved me back, really hard with both hands. He's much stronger than me and I'm only small like Amma, so it was much worse.

I fell into the big drain that runs along the side of the road. I twisted my ankle and landed right on my bottom which sent a pain shooting up my back. I bit my lip so hard I actually heard a crunch and tasted blood, _and_ I got all dirty from the disgusting drain.

I tried really hard not to cry, but I just couldn't help it. And I was SO ANGRY, I didn't even think. I just picked up a stone and threw it at him. But the stone missed him by miles and hit Alfie Bennet instead. He's only six. Poor thing screamed, and all the grown-ups crowded round him. There was blood on his head and it was all because of me, and I thought I'd killed him but I hadn't. I didn't admit to it because I was too scared. I was ashamed too, I suppose, but mostly I was scared of what I'd done and that I would get into trouble so I just pointed at David Hill and told everyone <u>he</u> threw the stone. Everyone believed me (of course they did!) because he was exactly the kind of boy who would throw stones.

Alfie Bennet was all right really. Just a graze on his head. He only cried for a minute before he went off to play with his friends as if nothing had happened. It wasn't like that for David Hill, though, because his papa was a 'nasty piece of work'. That's what Amma said, anyway. And everyone knew he used his belt on David if he got into trouble. Sometimes when David came to school, you could see him wince when he sat down. Or sometimes there were red marks across the back of his legs.

Mr Hill grabbed David's arm like he was going to break it. I think maybe it was worse than ever that day by the road because everyone was so scared and tired and confused - Mr Hill included.

Mr Hill dragged David right to the back of our group of cars where no one could see. David begged his papa. He was saying, 'Please. Please.' over and over again, and, 'Don't, Papa. No.' and it was horrible to hear. He tried to get away from him, but Mr Hill kept tight hold. Even Mrs Hill couldn't stop him from taking David behind the cars, and after a short while we heard Mr Hill's belt again and again and again. It sounded like when Dewi used to hang the mat on the line and beat the dust out of it with a bamboo beater.

Smack. Smack. Smack.

And David Hill was screaming, begging his papa to stop. All the other grown-ups turned away and looked at each other and no one said anything. I felt so sorry for David because it was my fault. Papa always says he hates lying and stealing and that honesty is the best policy but I had lied and I shouldn't have let David get into trouble for something I did. I shouldn't. I wanted to own up there and then but it was too late. It was too late for anything because all of a sudden there were car horns honking at the very back of the convoy. People further up the road were shouting and grabbing their children and scattering in all directions as if the end of the world was coming.

TWO DAYS UNTIL FULL MOON

28

POURING WORDS

Nisha couldn't go to the hidden garden the following day. Icy rain wrapped the island in a cold embrace. The wind howled. Heavy clouds scudded across the gloomy sky and thunder rumbled over the churning sea.

Barrow House hunched against the storm. Its dusky rooms and shadowy hallways slept uneasily. Its windows rattled and its roof tiles clattered like old bones.

Grandmother shut herself in the library with Humphrey, and Mrs F busied herself around the house and kitchen. Joy only came to the house in the evenings, so Nisha sat alone and watched over Amma, who shivered and suffered as her fever deepened.

Perched in the armchair in Amma's room, Nisha sat with a blanket over her knees to keep out the cold. On the table beside her, a lamp flickered against the dark day. The cocoon of orange light was just enough for her to see the writing spill from her pencil on to the lined pages of her journal.

Rain tapped on the window. Amma's breathing sighed in and out. The wind curled around the house.

Sometimes Nisha paused to watch Amma or pull at the itchy collar of her dress, but mostly she kept writing her truth because it really did help – just as Joy had said it might. Pouring the words on to the paper was like emptying poison from her mind. It made her feel lighter.

But there were thoughts gnawing at her that no amount of writing would cure.

Amma's sickness. Twig's bargain. The three lost treasures. And the certainty of the approaching full moon. Nisha was no closer to knowing what she had to find, or where to start looking. Her meeting with Twig was a half-remembered dream, and only the bracelet reassured her it had ever happened.

As she wrote and muddled through her thoughts, Nisha caught sight of something from the corner of her eye. A dark shadow leaning over Amma's bed. When she looked up, though, there was no one there. Before she could wonder if she had imagined it, Nisha felt a cold breath on her cheek.

She pulled away with a jolt. Her notebook and pencil fell from her knees and clattered on the floorboards.

The temperature in the room plummeted as if something had drained all the warmth from the world. Nisha's anxious breath puffed out in clouds.

Heart pounding, she grabbed the lamp and backed towards the window. Light shone into the dark corners, revealing an empty room, but gentle footsteps padded on the wooden floorboards. The numbing cold passed by as the footsteps moved towards the closed door where they paused as if waiting for Nisha to follow.

A moment later, there was soft running in the passageway outside. It continued towards the upper gallery then changed rhythm as if someone was descending a staircase. But it was too far away to be the main staircase leading down into the grand entrance hall.

Finally, the sound disappeared altogether and Nisha stayed as she was for a long time, staring at the door, trying to make sense of what had happened. She was certain she hadn't imagined it. *Was it Twig?* she wondered. *Could he come into the house?* Whatever it was, she had the strangest sense that it meant no harm, but that it was trying to entice her from the room.

Just then she heard footsteps again in the passageway. This time they were heavier. Coming closer, approaching the bedroom. Outside, the sky groaned and lightning flickered. It flashed bright inside the bedroom as the footsteps stopped and the doorknob rattled and turned.

As the door swung inwards, the sky rumbled long and loud. Lightning flashed again to reveal a figure standing in the dark passageway.

Nisha jumped with fright.

In the open doorway, Mrs F did the same.

'Eee, Lord!' said Mrs F, putting a hand to her chest. 'You almost made me jump out of my skin! What you doin' standing there like a ghost in the night?'

Nisha took a deep breath and lowered the lamp. 'I . . . I'm sorry.'

'Oh dearie, dearie me.' Mrs F calmed herself. 'Dearie me.'

'I'm really sorry,' Nisha said again. Her own heart was racing from the shock of seeing Mrs F standing there.

'Oh. Never mind pet.' Mrs F came in and placed a large bag beside the armchair. 'You just gave me a fright, that's all. The house can be a bit spooky sometimes. Especially on a stormy day like this. But I've got just the thing to take our minds off it.' She dipped into the bag and fished out a large bundle of wool. 'We're going to Knit for Victory.'

Nisha was still waiting for her heart to settle. Her mind was racing at a million miles per hour. 'Pardon?'

'The Women's Voluntary Service has organized a

knittin' circle in the village – a "work party" they're callin' it, though I've no idea why – and they're askin' all the ladies to knit socks and such for the soldiers. Some of the ladies even put little notes in. For the soldiers, that is.'

'I . . . I can't . . .'

'Divvent you be tellin' us you can't knit.' Mrs F rolled her eyes. 'They're not askin' us to build aeroplanes, pet, just knit a few socks. If I can do it, I'm sure a clever young thing like you can learn to do it.'

But Nisha decided there and then that she wasn't going to knit any socks. Those mysterious footsteps had meant something. They wanted her to leave the bedroom for a reason and she was beginning to suspect she knew why. She had an important job to do, and time was running out. Instead of waiting for the three lost treasures to appear, it was time to go on a hunt. She would explore the house from top to bottom, and she would find them.

'Can I learn later?' she asked. 'I need to stretch my legs for a bit. Get some exercise.'

'There's nee gannin' outside on a day like this,' Mrs F warned.

'Just around the house, then.' Nisha gathered her things and headed for the door. 'I think it would do me good.'

'Aye, well.' Mrs F sighed. 'All reet, pet, but stay away

from the study – if you get under Mrs Barrow's feet she'll have yer guts for garters.'

But Nisha was already in the passageway before Mrs F had finished her sentence.

29

THE SEARCH BEGINS

Nisha quickly learnt that it's almost impossible to find something when you don't know what you're looking for.

She started on the ground floor, rummaging through kitchen cupboards and drawers. She even clawed through the dirty washing in the scullery, and peered behind the mangle to find only an elaborate web with a fat spider sitting at the centre of it.

As she explored further, she discovered that nothing about Barrow House made sense. She opened stiff doors that led to gloomy passageways she didn't know existed. She found sad rooms and empty cupboards that didn't want to be found. She discovered creaky staircases designed to allow servants to come and go without being seen. And doors swung shut behind her.

In those murky passageways and dusty rooms, it was easy to believe in ghosts. Cocooned in the glow of her lamp, Nisha imagined lost souls pushing in from the shadows. She felt their watchful gaze. She heard footsteps and muffled voices vibrating in the walls and ceilings. But although she was filled with discomfort and dread, she was determined to keep looking. So she held her lamp high and pressed on while the storm wailed outside.

She investigated the parlour, the sitting room, the boot room, the games room, on and on until only one downstairs room remained unchecked – her grandmother's study. But Nisha knew it would be impossible to explore because Grandmother spent so much time in there.

However, as she was about to head upstairs, Nisha stepped into a pocket of cold air that made her stop dead. It was exactly like it had been in the bedroom earlier – as if all the warmth had been stolen from the world. As if something unearthly had enveloped her.

She stood with one foot on the staircase, one hand on the bannister, hardly daring to move. Her breath puffed out in small clouds.

A soft creak from behind made her glance over her shoulder to see that the study door was now ajar.

Light filtered through the narrow crack, giving Nisha a direct view of Grandmother's desk. The chair behind it was empty.

Nisha waited at the foot of the staircase, watching.

The cold shrunk around her, tightening its grip, then released her and drew away. Soft footsteps sounded on the stone floor and then, as if encouraged by an invisible hand, the study door eased open a little further. Just enough to see there was no one in the room.

Afraid, Nisha looked about. When she did so, she caught a glimpse of something from the corner of her eye; a shadow by the study door. But, as before in the bedroom, when she turned to look directly at the place where the shadow had been, there was nothing to see.

Nothing except for the study door standing open, inviting her inside to investigate.

A sense of calm came over Nisha, as it had done when she was near the Weeping Tree. She suddenly felt certain that she needed to see inside that room. If she was going to find Twig's three lost treasures, she had to search *everywhere*. Even her grandmother's study.

So Nisha hurried across the hallway and slipped inside.

30

DEADHEAD

Mrs Barrow's study was about the size of Nisha's bedroom, with a large window at the far end. Heavy curtains hung either side of it, and rain tip-tapped like spectral fingers drumming on the glass. In front of the window, facing the door, was a wide desk, carved from mahogany and topped with green leather. A single armchair and side table occupied one corner of the room, with an old basket full of hair-mottled blankets slumped beside them.

The room smelt of damp dog, flowers and dusty paper.

Nisha moved quietly on the worn carpet. She held the lamp high and passed by the shelves that lined each wall, running her fingertips along the spines of the leather-bound books. They were all different colours, like dull jewels. Red. Green. Black. Blue. The comforting odour of musty pages lifted into the air, and Nisha felt at peace there.

It didn't surprise Nisha to find the surface of the desk neat and organized. A small stack of letters on one side, a pile of papers on the other. Pen and ink were left clean and ready for use. Beside them was a crystal vase of sweet-smelling, pink daphne stems.

There was a photograph too.

Nisha held the lamp closer to see the black-and-white image of four people in front of Barrow House. There was no mistaking her grandmother. She looked younger, and softer in the face, but it was definitely her. She was wearing a pale dress, and a large hat, and sitting on what looked like one of the dining room chairs. On her right, perched on the arm of the chair, was a boy wearing a formal suit. Papa. He must have been about twelve years old when the photograph was taken – almost the same age Nisha was now. Standing to Grandmother's left was a skinny girl wearing a high-collared dress. Behind her, with one hand on her shoulder, was a man. Nisha supposed he was Mr Barrow. Her grandfather.

But it was the girl who caught Nisha's interest.

Her gaze was drawn to the girl's blazing eyes and sharp cheekbones. To her short hair that fell in dark waves. To her stormy expression.

There was something familiar about her, and Nisha found herself wondering whether this photograph was important to Twig. It was the only interesting thing she had found so far.

'Is this it, Twig?' Nisha whispered. 'Is this what you want me to find?'

'What did you say?'

Nisha looked up to see her grandmother standing in the doorway. She had been so lost in thought she hadn't heard her approach. 'I . . .'

Humphrey scooted across to greet Nisha. He jumped up and put his wet front paws on her knees, but Nisha ignored him.

'I . . . I'm sorry,' she blurted. 'I shouldn't have come in, I just—'

'What were you saying?' her grandmother asked.

'Nothing,' Nisha said. 'I was . . .' She thought quickly. 'Just thinking aloud.' She couldn't repeat it. She had promised not to breathe a word about Twig or their agreement.

'I see.' Grandmother narrowed her eyes in suspicion. She stood like that for a moment then came towards the desk. 'Humphrey, bed.'

Humphrey scurried away and, with a groan, flopped into the basket beside the armchair.

'I'm . . . sorry,' Nisha said. 'The door was open.'

'That's the draught,' said Mrs Barrow. 'Forever

blowing the door open. I must get Mr Foster to look at it for me.'

'I should go,' Nisha said, but before she could escape, her grandmother came to stand beside her.

Mrs Barrow peered down at Nisha, her expression softening as some thought or another soothed her. And then, as if an unheard voice had caught her attention, she sighed and turned towards the window that faced the north end of Barrow Island. Through the rain they could see the silhouette of the Keep, and the Weeping Tree standing close by.

'I'm surprised that tree is still standing,' Grandmother said.

She sounded sad instead of angry, and Nisha watched her, trying to read the expression in her eyes.

'I just can't quite bring myself to . . .' Mrs Barrow stopped herself. 'It's a pity it's raining. I should have liked to go to the garden today, but the most I can manage is to take Humphrey out for a few minutes. Perhaps we could go together some time. To the garden, that is. I can tell you the names of the flowers.'

'I'd like that,' Nisha said. 'Amm— Mother would like it too. She loves flowers.'

'And when the roses come, I can show you how to prune and deadhead them.'

Nisha nodded, even though she had no idea what that meant.

Grandmother stared out at the rain. 'I'm sorry I'm not better company for you. And I'm sorry your mother isn't any better yet. I imagine you're very worried about her, but I have instructed Doctor Michaels to do everything he can. I'd like her to be well when your father returns.'

Nisha looked up at her with sudden excitement. 'Have you heard something? Is he coming?'

'I'm afraid not,' Grandmother said. 'Not yet.'

Nisha's face fell.

'But I'm confident we shall see him again.' Grandmother looked down at her with a sad smile. 'We must never give up hope. You see, sometimes hope is all we have.'

ONE DAY UNTIL FULL MOON

31
THE HIDDEN ROOM

After lunch on the first day of searching the house, Mrs F insisted she reach Nisha to knit. They spent the rest of that rainy afternoon in Amma's room in a tangle of grey wool. When Joy came that evening, soaked through to the bone, Nisha didn't want to miss a moment in her company, so she had to wait until the next day before she could continue her search of Barrow House.

The rain persisted through the night and into the following morning, and when Nisha checked on Amma before breakfast, she was shocked to learn that the fever had worsened. Amma's face was gaunt. Her skin was tight and her eyes had sunk deep into their sockets. Her temperature was so high, Nisha could feel the heat burning off her. Joy went back to the mainland and sent for Doctor Michaels but when he came and examined Amma, he said there was nothing he could do until the right medication arrived from Newcastle. The only thing left was to try keeping her cool with damp flannels and fresh air.

And to find three lost treasures, Nisha thought.

She was determined now, more than ever, that she must find them right away.

Mrs F insisted she have breakfast, so Nisha stuffed down a boiled egg and a slice of toast, then took a lamp and set about her search once more.

The layout upstairs was just as confusing as it was downstairs. Some bedrooms opened into other bedrooms. There were large, empty dressing rooms, and balconies at both the front and back of the house. There were concealed passageways with staircases leading up from downstairs.

Nisha checked everything – even creeping into her grandmother's bedroom – but found nothing of interest.

Until she found the secret door.

It was hiding at the back of the main gallery that overlooked the hallway. Tucked away in one corner, the door was cut into the wooden panels, with a recessed handle that blended in perfectly. It was easy to overlook in the gloomy house, but as soon as she passed it, she felt the same icy grip she had felt the day before. The cold drew Nisha to the door as if it were leading her there. As if it wanted her to find it.

Nisha slipped her fingers into the recess and pulled the door open to reveal a staircase spiralling upwards. She remembered the footsteps she had heard yesterday outside her door. She had thought they were heading downstairs, but perhaps they had been heading up.

Nisha held the lamp high and climbed the first step. She felt the temperature drop further. The freezing air tickled her skin into gooseflesh and seeped deep into the marrow of her bones. She stopped and took a moment to crush her doubts about climbing the cold staircase, then tightened her jaw and continued.

Her boots scuffed on the stone steps. Her breath puffed around her like steam. The lamplight cast eerie shadows on the darkening walls as she followed the staircase that twisted upwards before reaching a small carpeted landing with just one door.

The brass handle was like ice. Nisha could hardly bear to touch it as she twisted and pushed, but the door was locked.

Shivering, she blew warm breath on her fingers and pulled the sleeve of her dress over her hand before trying the handle again.

Definitely locked.

She pressed her ear to the wood, but heard nothing from inside, then she crouched and put her eye to the keyhole.

She couldn't see much. It was murky inside. She could just about make out the corner of a bed, but that was all. Something prickled at the back of her head. Like tiny ants crawling across her scalp. Nisha began to suspect there was something important in this room. It was the only locked door she had found.

She got down on her hands and knees. She turned her head sideways, pressed her cheek hard against the carpet and tried to look under the door. There was a good-sized gap, but all she could see was the edge of a rug, and the legs of a bed, with a counterpane hanging down.

Nisha stood up and tried the door again as if it might have magically opened, but it was still locked.

She had to get in there. It had to be important. She was beginning to think that whatever Twig was looking for, it was inside this locked room.

'What are you up to?' The voice took her by surprise and Nisha stepped away from the door. She turned to see Mrs F standing at the top of the staircase, with a pile of clothes in her arms. Nisha hadn't heard her footsteps. She had been caught red-handed.

'Get away from there,' said Mrs F. 'This place isn't for you.'

Nisha noticed that Mrs F was holding a key in one hand. There was a brown label attached to it with a piece of string.

'What's in there?' Nisha asked. 'Why is it locked?' She noticed that her breath was no longer like steam. The soul-aching cold had gone.

'That's none of your beeswax,' said Mrs F. 'Mrs Barrow wants it kept locked, so locked it stays. More than me job's worth to say any more.'

'But, I just—'

'No "justs" or "buts". That room is out of bounds to anyone but Mrs Barrow.'

'I—'

'I divvent want to hear it. Now, get away from there.' Mrs F beckoned. 'Gan and wait for us in your mam's bedroom. I've got summat to keep you out of trouble.'

Sitting on the stool in Amma's room, with a bundle of old socks at her feet, and Mrs F humming in the chair, Nisha was fed up and full of worry. She was trying to darn a hole in the toe of a sock – after yesterday's tangle, they had decided she wasn't ready for actual knitting yet – but she was finding it difficult to concentrate. She kept looking at Amma and thinking that her fever was getting worse while she, Nisha, was just sitting there doing nothing but knitting. And every time Nisha moved her hand, she felt the bracelet tight around her wrist – a constant reminder of her agreement with Twig, and that time was running out.

Nisha hadn't yet found anything Twig might want, and if she didn't find the three treasures in time, Amma might die and she might never see Papa again. More and more, she thought about the locked room. More and more, she became convinced that she had to see inside it. It was the only place she hadn't searched. She *had* to know what was in there. But how on earth would she ever get in?

'Divvent make a mess o' that sock,' Mrs F said. When she spoke, she shifted in the armchair, revealing a corner of brown card sticking out of the pocket on the front of her apron. Nisha immediately remembered what Mrs F had been holding outside the locked room, and she stared at that little corner of brown card, thinking about the key that was attached to it. She wondered if it was the key to the locked room. And if it *was*, then was there a way to take it without Mrs F noticing?

'It's stopped raining,' Mrs F said.

'Hmm?' Nisha glanced up, trying not to look guilty. She had been thinking about stealing the key, and that made her nervous. Stealing was, of course, wrong.

'I said it's *finally* stopped raining.'

'Oh.' Nisha glanced out of the window.

Mrs F smiled. 'So why not put down that darning and get yoursel' outside? I know Mrs Barrow prefers you inside, but you must be gaspin' for some fresh air after two days locked up with me. I'm sure it'll be fine so long as you stay clear of the north end. And she did say it would be all right for you to sit in the flower garden.'

32

A FACE AT THE WINDOW

The ground was damp underfoot, and a rich earthy smell rose from the grass around the house. With her notebook tucked into her pocket, Nisha took the path up to the walled garden, where she intended to sit among the flowers and write more of her thoughts. Maybe she would even come up with a way to get that key from Mrs F, or think of another way into that locked room.

Halfway along the path, Nisha felt a curious prickling at the nape of her neck. In that instant, she was certain someone was watching her. Nisha stopped in her tracks and looked back at the house. Movement flickered, making her lift her eyes to a large bay window jutting out from the roof at the back of Barrow House. Her first thought was how odd it was she hadn't noticed the window before.

Her second thought was that the window belonged to the locked room.

Thick curtains were drawn across the glass, but as Nisha watched, fingers curled around the edge of one curtain. They tightened and pulled the heavy material to one side, just a fraction. There was nothing but darkness in the gap. An emptiness, as if there were no room behind it at all; only a void of never-ending night. The disembodied fingers remained still. Pale and ghostly against the curtains. Then something moved in the void.

An eerie feeling washed over Nisha. Her eyes widened and her scalp tightened as she watched the face materialize out of the abyss between the curtains. Pallid and indistinct at this distance, it was impossible to make out any features. Only dark hollows where the shadows lay across the face.

Nisha slipped her hand into her pocket and gripped the red stone. She took a half-step back, wondering if it was Twig. Was he watching her? Or was someone else up there? Some*thing* else? Nisha couldn't tear her gaze from that shadowy face. She was locked to it, as if it would never let her go.

But then a gull screamed high in the grey sky. The

sharp cry cut through her thoughts like a blunt saw. It was joined by others so that the air above the island was filled with the crazed laughter of gulls. Nisha blinked, then caught sight of something moving to her left. Something close to the ground.

She whipped around to see a skinny boy dart through the long grass and disappear behind a gorse bush.

'Twig?' She left the path. 'Is that you?' As she came closer, she saw that he was crouched behind the gorse, not doing a very good job of hiding. 'Is it you?'

'What did you call me?' Jamie stood up and raised his eyebrows. 'Are you sayin' I'm skinny?'

Nisha was disappointed. She had wanted to see Twig and get some clue about what she was supposed to find for him.

'What are you doing here?' she asked. 'You're not supposed to be here.'

'Why not?'

'My grandmother doesn't like people coming on to the island.' She looked back at the house, checking the window, but the curtain was now in place, and the face was gone.

'I know, but I'm not just "people", am I?' Jamie said. 'I'm the one that saved your life, remember?'

'*She* doesn't know that. And she's only just starting to like me – *sort of* – so I don't want to give her more reasons to hate me.'

Jamie sniffed hard, making a snorting noise. 'Why would she hate ya?'

Nisha thought about it for a moment. She didn't like to say it out loud because it made it feel more real. 'Because she thinks my papa should have married a nice English girl. Because I'm brown, I suppose, instead of white like you.'

Jamie smirked.

'What's funny about that?' Nisha asked.

'Your "papa"? Sounds geet posh. You mean your da'?'

'Yes.'

Jamie sat down on the wet grass, not caring that his shorts immediately darkened as the material soaked up the rain. 'You still got them sweets?' he asked. 'Me mam won't let us have any.'

Nisha fished them from her pocket, brushing her fingers against the red stone. Every time she touched it, her mind was transported back to that last perfect morning in Malaya, sitting under the jambu tree in front of the house with the sun high in the sky. It made her heart ache.

She offered them to Jamie, who took a cola cube.

'You not havin' one?' he asked.

Nisha's throat was still sore from when she had almost choked to death a few days ago.

'Gan on. Have a pear drop. They're me next best favourite.' He put his grubby fingers into the bag, took out a pear-shaped pink sweet coated with a dusting of sugar, and offered it to Nisha. 'Gan on.'

Nisha looked at Jamie's fingernails, trying not to grimace.

'What?' Jamie asked. 'You lookin' at me clarty fingers? Aye, well, I was collectin' manure on the farm. Big sloppy country pancakes.'

'Oh.' Nisha recoiled in horror.

Jamie cracked up with a loud laugh. 'I'm pullin' your leg, man. It's just everyday dirt. Gan on, have a sweet.'

Nisha shook her head. 'No, thanks.'

Jamie stood up. 'Suit yersel'. I'll have it later.' He stuffed the pear drop into his pocket. 'So. Are ya gonna take me to the tree?'

'Get down!' Nisha hissed.

'It's fine. There's nee one about.'

Nisha glanced up at the house, watching the window at the top. The curtains were still covering the window, but she thought she had seen them move again.

'There's someone up there,' she said.

'Where?'

'Top window,' Nisha said without pointing. 'I saw the curtains move.'

Jamie squinted. 'I divvent see nowt. You're imaginin' it.'

'I'm not.'

'Maybe it's a ghost, then,' Jamie said. 'Wouldn't be

surprised if this place is haunted. Have you seen any ghosts?'

'No,' Nisha said. 'Never.'

'Shame. That would be excitin'.' Jamie watched the top window for a while longer. 'Howay then, let's gan to the tree. We can make a wish.'

'I don't think—'

'You promised,' Jamie said. 'I saved your life, remember?'

'I don't remember promising anything.'

'Aye, you did.' Jamie took Nisha's arm and started pulling her along the path.

Nisha sighed. 'All right, but stay out of sight. If anyone sees us, we're in big trouble.'

Mr Hill was still beating David when people started to realize what was happening further up the convoy. Then panic started to spread from one group to another. People were suddenly shouting and running into the jungle on either side of the road. Some cars were leaving the convoy and speeding past in a cloud of dust. Even army vehicles were hurrying past. I didn't know what was happening until Papa said, 'Dear God, it's them,' and I looked up into the evening sky between the trees and saw all these tiny black specks in the distance that were getting bigger and bigger.

It was too late for us to get in the car and drive away.

'This way!' Papa shouted, and we sprinted across the road towards the drainage ditch. Already there were people lying there, face down in the dirt and the sewage, with their hands over their heads.

'Hurry!' Papa shouted. 'Get in!'

The noise of planes was getting louder and louder and Papa sounded scared so we jumped into the ditch and lay as flat as we could. Amma was beside me, and Papa was lying on top of us for protection, just like when we were in the banyan tree.

'Dive bombers!' someone said. 'Keep your heads down!' But I couldn't help looking up to see the planes getting closer. There were cars all over the road and people still running in different directions searching for somewhere to hide. They were diving into the drain, or heading into the jungle, or ducking behind cars and trucks. Some people didn't have time to find anywhere so they just got down flat on the road, trying to protect their children with their arms. That's when I saw David Hill and his parents climbing into the drain further along from where we were.

After that, the shooting started.

The planes dived down at us with a ghastly scream and a stuttering rat-tat-tat-tat of machine guns. I'd never heard anything so awful. Columns of dirt and dust spurted up from the road and the cars bounced and shook as the bullets ripped into them. Then there was a great roar as the first plane flew right over our heads. It was followed by a terrifying BOOM! as a truck exploded in a ball of orange fire. I felt a burning flash of heat and the whole truck lifted off the ground and spun across the road to hit the trees at the edge of the jungle. The ground shook. People screamed. Trees were on fire and the whole world became fuzzy. The air was filled with dust and dirt.

The attack went on and on. It lasted for ever and ever, and even when it was over, it felt as if it wasn't.

My ears were ringing. My head was numb. My eyes were full of dust, and my mouth was full of grit. But that wasn't the worst of it. The worst was what I saw afterwards. I never want to see anything like that again. Not <u>ever</u>.

33
WISHES

The easiest way to the Weeping Tree was through the walled garden and out the other side. The path was overgrown, but at least it led straight up to the Keep. There was no way Nisha was going to take Jamie that way, though. There was a good chance Mr Foster would be working in the garden now the rain had stopped, and Nisha's grandmother might be in the flower garden.

'We'll have to go all the way round,' Nisha said. 'Come on.' She began picking her way through the gorse towards the seaward side of the island.

As they went, Nisha felt as if Barrow House was watching her from behind its dark, drawn curtains. The sooner she was out of sight of that top window, the better.

The smell of the sea grew stronger as they came closer to the narrow beach that appeared at low tide, and soon they were on the dunes and running down to the sand.

'This is amazing!' Jamie said. 'You got your own beach, wi' nee one to bother you.' He sprinted down to the surf.

Nisha stopped on the sand by the grassy dunes as if she had reached an invisible wall. Her chest tightened and her breathing became shallow. She closed her eyes and concentrated hard to not imagine how it would feel to be stranded out there in the sea. To be pushed down where there was only darkness and the burn of salt water in her lungs.

Down and down into the dark.

'I bet you come plodgin' here all the time.' Jamie jumped back as a wave washed in and covered the toes of his boots. 'It must be brilliant in the summer.' He came running back to Nisha like an overexcited dog.

'I haven't been here in the summer.' Nisha shivered and took a deep breath. She forced herself to look out at the water, but even just that made her stomach sick.

'D'you get the seals comin' up on the sand?' Jamie asked. 'I bet you do. I bet you get seals.'

'I don't know. Maybe.'

'An' I bet it's amazin' ridin' your pony along here.

What's she called? Hell's bells, you must love gallopin' in the surf.'

'I can't ride.'

'Then I'll teach ya.' Jamie couldn't hide his excitement. 'I'm half gypsy, y'knaa? Ridin' ponies is in me blood. I'm a *brilliant* rider.'

'If you say so.'

'Wait.' Jamie's excitement fell away. 'D'you not believe us? I'm not showin' off, y'knaa? It's the truth.'

'All right.'

'It *is*,' Jamie insisted. 'Ask anyone.'

'I don't really care.' Nisha turned away from the sea.

'What's the matter?' Jamie saw the expression on Nisha's face. 'You look scared.'

Nisha couldn't help stealing a glance at the waves.

Down and down into the dark.

'Is it the water?' he asked. 'Are you frightened of the water?'

'No.'

'Can you not swim? I can teach ya.'

'Of course I can swim,' Nisha said. 'I just . . . I don't like the *sea*.'

'Oh.' Jamie frowned. 'Well, I s'pose it can be a bit scary but why—'

'I don't want to talk about it.'

Jamie watched her with a serious expression, then burst out laughing. He opened his mouth so wide that

Nisha saw the cola cube between his back teeth.

'What?' Nisha glared at him. 'What's so funny?'

'Nothin'.' He put a hand over his mouth to stop himself. 'It's just; you live on an island, and you're scared of the sea. That's tough luck, that is.'

At the end of the beach, the land rose towards the crag at the north of the island. The climb was gentle at first, but soon became much steeper. Sometimes rocky, sometimes soft and grassy.

They clambered up and up, often forced to move on all fours as they made their way to the top. Higher and higher. They were out of sight of the rest of the island. All they could see was the water below them on one side, and rocks and gorse on the other.

But Nisha could already feel the call of the Weeping Tree.

She felt it deep in her bones, like a steady hum that sang through her.

'Do you feel anything?' she asked Jamie when they stopped to catch their breath.

'Like what?'

'I don't know. Nothing.' If he *did* feel it, he would know what she was talking about.

When they reached the top, they climbed the final rise of a grassy bank and found themselves close to the crag.

A little further along, and they would be at the point where the island fell away in a steep cliff to the sea far below.

From where they stood, the house was still out of sight, but Nisha could see the upper half of the ruined Keep, and the very top of the Weeping Tree.

'I see it.' Jamie picked up his pace. 'I see the tree.'

They hurried along the crag, Nisha being careful to stay away from the edge, and soon they were standing beneath the outstretched branches.

Nisha had never been so close to it in daylight.

A week ago, when she had sat beneath it, moonlight washing over her, the breath of the wind had been gentle and she had felt calm. Safe. But now the wind was blustering, and she felt anything but calm. Being this close to the edge of the crag was terrifying. Her hands were sweating and her legs felt weak. Her stomach churned like the grey sea that smashed on the rocks far below.

'So this is it.' Jamie wasn't bothered by the long drop just beyond the thick roots. He stood with his hands on his hips looking up at the underside of the tree house wedged in the palm of the old tree.

'Can you get inside?' he asked.

Nisha hardly dared look away from the edge. It made her queasy to see it, and all she could think about was how it would feel to drop over, but she couldn't look away.

'I bet you can,' Jamie said. 'I bet you can get in—'

'No.' The thought of it broke the spell. 'You can't.'

'Why not?'

'It's too dangerous.' Nisha looked up at the underside of the tree house, where a trapdoor rattled in the wind. A short length of frayed rope ladder hung down from it, but it was too high to reach. 'You can't go up. It's too windy. Imagine if it blew the tree house too hard. It might come loose and tumble over . . .' Nisha glanced towards the edge again. Over the sound of the wind she could just about make out the muffled crash of the waves below.

'Maybe I can just make my wish here.' Jamie closed his eyes tight. His whole face scrunched.

'What did you wish for?' Nisha asked when he opened his eyes again.

'Wishes divvent come true if you tell someone. Everyone knows that.'

The wind whistled through the gaps in the walls of the tree house above them. Nisha could feel the vibrations running right through the trunk and into the roots just below her feet.

'Nothing feels any different,' Jamie said. 'I divvent think it worked.'

'We should go,' Nisha told him. 'Back down to the beach, where no one can see us.'

'Maybe I have to climb up there.' Jamie reached for

the lowest branch. 'Maybe I need to be up there for it to come true.'

'No!' Nisha tried to stop him, but he jumped to grab the branch and pulled himself up.

'Stop,' Nisha pleaded with him. 'It's dangerous. And you'll get us into trouble.'

But Jamie climbed higher, moving from branch to branch until there were fewer and fewer handholds.

'Stop it! Get down here!'

'I bet I can get inside the tree house,' Jamie said. He was high up now. His dark hair was flicking about, and the hems of his shorts were flapping. The branches were swaying dramatically, and Nisha was sure the wind was getting worse. It moaned through the tree, scattering dead twigs that broke from the highest branches. The tree house creaked and groaned. The trapdoor rattled as if something was trying to escape.

'Get down!' Nisha said again, and when Jamie stopped climbing, there was a moment when she thought he was going to do it. But instead, he reached out, stretching for the frayed rope ladder that hung from the underside of the tree house.

But it was too far and he lost his balance.

His feet slipped on the wet bark and he snatched hold of the nearest branch to stop himself from falling.

'That was close,' he said, looking down at Nisha. 'But I reckon I can get in through the window if I climb higher.'

'No,' Nisha said. 'Just come down. *Please.*'

'I can get up this way.' Jamie turned and began shuffling along a thick branch that protruded from the tree, stretching out towards the edge of the crag. 'I see a place to climb higher.'

It made Nisha feel sick just to watch him shuffling closer and closer to the drop. If he tumbled and went over, he'd fall into the churning sea below.

Down and down into the dark.

The angry waves would dash him to pieces on the rocks and—

'Get down from there! What on earth do you think you're doing!' The wind died in an instant, as if it had been turned off with a switch.

'Get down at once!' The voice came again as Nisha turned to see her grandmother striding along the overgrown path like a sergeant major at a parade. There was fire and fury in her eyes. Her right hand was raised in a shaking fist. 'Get down!'

For the next few seconds, everything passed slowly, as if in a dream.

Nisha saw her grandmother coming along the path, shouting, then she heard a gasp of surprise from behind her. When she turned back to the tree, Jamie was falling. He had lost his balance when he looked up to see Mrs Barrow, and his feet skidded on the moss-mottled wet bark. He came down with his legs either side of the wide branch.

'Oof!'

It would have been funny if he hadn't been on a branch that was reaching out over the crag. Because of that, it was terrifying.

Jamie tried to hang on as he toppled sideways. He hugged the branch with both arms but he just slid round and his legs dropped so that he was dangling over the edge of the crag.

He looked across at Nisha, eyes wide because he knew what was about to happen. His fingers were slipping on the slimy bark. He struggled hard, kicking his legs backwards and forwards, trying to get hold of something. Anything.

And then he lost his grip altogether.

Instead of falling straight down, he jerked forward while he was in mid-air. It was as if something had grabbed hold of him and yanked him forward. Legs wheeling, Jamie plummeted to the ground. He crashed through small branches too weak to hold or stop him, and hit the roots of the Weeping Tree with a bone-crunching thump.

For a moment, Nisha thought that was it. He had landed with a bump but he would be all right.

But she was wrong. When Jamie hit the tree roots, he bounced, tumbled sideways, and slipped over the edge of the crag.

34
OVER THE EDGE

Nisha wanted to help, but the thought of going anywhere near the edge made her heart stop and start erratically. Her head swam and the world spun around her. She stepped backwards, not daring to go closer, not wanting to see that Jamie was gone.

'Mr Foster!' Nisha's grandmother was running in the other direction now, returning to the garden. She was shouting at the top of her voice. 'Mr Foster! Help! Help!'

Humphrey ran around her ankles, barking as if it were a game.

Before she reached the wall to the secluded garden, Mr Foster appeared from behind the curtain of ivy.

'This way!' Nisha's grandmother pointed towards the crag. Towards the place where Nisha was standing, frozen by fear.

'A boy,' Grandmother was saying. 'A boy went over.'

Mr Foster ran past her, coming along the path with a thumping of boots. There was a breath of air as he rushed past Nisha, then he went right to the edge to look over.

Humphrey followed, scuttling dangerously close to the edge.

'Get back here!' Grandmother called to him. 'Heel!' She picked him up and went to stand beside Nisha. All the colour had gone from her face. She was pale as moon-light. Her eyes were wide and filled with tears, and she had one hand on her mouth as if she were trying to hold something in.

Nisha had seen horrible things during her evacuation from Malaya. She had seen terror in people's eyes, and she knew she was seeing it again, right now, in her grand-mother's eyes. Pure, cold terror.

On the crag, Mr Foster was shouting.

'Hold on, boy!'

It took Nisha a second to process what he had said. *Hold on*. That must mean that Jamie hadn't fallen into the sea. Perhaps he had found something to cling to.

Mr Foster unfastened his belt. He slipped it from the loops on his trousers and wrapped it once around his hand. The action brought a poisonous memory bubbling to the surface in Nisha's mind. For a moment she was transported back on to the road to Singapore, with David Hill's screams in her ears. But Mr Foster was using his belt for a noble purpose; he tightened his fist around it and got down on his front in the wet grass at the lip of the crag. He hung his arms over the edge.

'Be careful, Bill!' Mrs Barrow clamped one hand on Nisha's shoulder and squeezed.

On the crag, Mr Foster's whole body tensed and it looked as if he might slide forward and topple over the edge too. Nisha wanted to run to help him, but her feet were stuck to the spot. It was as if fear was a real, living thing that grew inside her. It had put out its roots and burrowed into the ground to hold her in place. She couldn't move.

And then Mr Foster dug the toes of his boots into the soft ground and used his elbows to stop himself. He started to shuffle backwards. His whole body was trembling with strain, but neither Nisha nor her grandmother made any attempt to help. They simply stood there, staring in horror as Mr Foster finally managed to drag himself away from the edge of the crag.

And when his fist came into view, Nisha saw that the leather belt was still there. It was pulled taut as if there were something heavy on the end.

Mr Foster drew himself up on to his knees and took

hold of the belt with both hands, tugging hard. That's when Jamie's small pale hand came into view, followed by his arm. And when the top of Jamie's head appeared, Mr Foster grabbed the back of Jamie's coat and hauled him to safety.

The two of them collapsed in the wet grass, heaving for breath.

35
MASTER KEY

Nisha was surprised her grandmother didn't tell them off and start shouting at them as soon as she knew Jamie was safe. Instead, she put Humphrey down without a word and turned towards Nisha, about to hug her. But then she stopped herself and lowered her arms. It was as if, for a moment, a door had opened somewhere inside Mrs Barrow, but she had closed it before any warmth could escape.

She was still bone-pale when she spoke to Mr Foster, and she couldn't hide the tremble in her voice. 'Well done, Bill. Are you all right?'

'I'm canny, Mrs Barrow. Got a fright, that's all. This

poor lad's worse off than me.'

'Can you get him back to the house?' Grandmother spoke quietly.

'Aye.' Mr Foster scooped Jamie into his arms as if he were a puppy, and started back along the path.

Nisha's grandmother looked back at the tree standing on the crag. She put her fingers to her mouth and let out a strange sound. Nisha thought then, that her grandmother suddenly looked very old. Her hands shook. Her lips trembled. Her face was drained of colour and her stern strength was gone.

'Should we send for Doctor Michaels?' Mrs Barrow said as if the thought had just occurred to her. She turned and went after Mr Foster. 'We should send for him straight away.'

'I divvent think we need the doc,' said Mr Foster. 'Mrs F will clean him up.'

'But what if he's hurt? What if—'

'He's fine. Just shook up like you are. A few cuts 'n' bruises that'll be right with a bit of cleaning. I'll hoy the kettle on and make some tea while Mrs F cleans him up.'

'Tea?' Mrs Barrow sounded confused. 'Tea? Yes. Yes, tea would be nice. That'll help.'

So they went through the walled garden, back to the house.

Jamie sat on a stool while Mrs F cleaned his cuts and

scrapes using so much Dettol antiseptic that the whole scullery started to smell like a hospital. She tutted and shook her head while she was doing it.

Nisha's grandmother was still trembling. Some of the colour had finally come back to her face, but she looked smaller than Nisha remembered. She stayed with them long enough to make sure that Jamie was all right, then retreated to her study. Her voice wavered when she said she needed to sit down and collect her thoughts.

Mr Foster went into the kitchen to boil the kettle. 'Nowt makes things better like a cup of tea,' he said.

'I divvent think it needs stitches.' Mrs F wiped the cut on Jamie's shin. It was a long gash, with blood welling up from it. Every time Mrs F wiped it away, more oozed out. 'But it's going to take a while to stop bleeding. Here, hold this tight.' She took one of Jamie's hands and put it over the cloth to press against the cut. 'Divvent take it away until it stops.'

Nisha stood back, trying to stay out of Mrs F's way. Any minute now, someone was going to start shouting at her. They had told her so many times to stay away from the Weeping Tree, and what had she done? She had gone to the tree, and now look what had happened. She wasn't going to get away without someone shouting at her.

'Does your mam knaa you're here on the island, Jamie Harper?' asked Mrs F.

Jamie shook his head and looked at the stone floor.

He was shivering so much his teeth chattered. Mrs F said it was shock, and Nisha wasn't surprised.

'You're lucky to be alive,' Mrs F said as she wrung out a cloth and dabbed at another of Jamie's wounds. 'And so is Mr Foster from the sound of it. What on earth were you thinkin'?'

Here it comes, Nisha thought. But as she took another step back, she glanced up at the row of hooks beside the large stone sink. Each one was no bigger than her curled little finger, and there were all kinds of things hanging from them – a dog lead, an old flannel, a rusty chain. But it was a large, black, ancient-looking key that caught Nisha's attention. Previously, she had seen it in Mrs F's hand, and then in her pocket, but now it was right there on the hook. Attached to it by a short length of string was a piece of creased brown card with something written on it. The handwriting was spidery and difficult to read, but once Nisha worked out what it said, it was obvious.

Master Key

Those two words were like a bright light switching on in her head. Nisha had been right. The key *was* her way into the locked room.

'I divvent knaa what you two were playin' at . . .' Mrs F was saying, but Nisha wasn't listening. Her eyes were fixed on the key. It could lead to the three treasures that would save Amma and Papa. She had to take it.

Nisha edged around the scullery until she was directly behind Mrs F.

'How many times have you been telt not to gan anywhere near that tree?' Still on her knees, Mrs F was far too busy cleaning Jamie's cuts and scrapes to notice what Nisha was doing.

Nisha watched the back of the housekeeper's head, waiting for just the right moment, and then she reached out. She put her fingers on the key and—

'What do you think you're deein'?'

Nisha whipped her hand away as Mrs F turned around to look at her.

'Eh?' Mrs F raised her eyebrows.

'Pardon?'

'I asked what you two clots thought you was deein', gannin' up there and larkin' about by the tree. It's out of bounds and you know it. Fetch me some clean water.' She moved to one side and pushed the basin across the stone floor towards Nisha. The scraping-screeching sound was like nails down a blackboard.

'Hurry up.' Mrs F glared at her.

Splashing bloody water on the floor, Nisha managed to pick up the basin and carry it to the sink. She tipped it away and drew more from the small handpump.

When Nisha put the clean water down beside Mrs F, the housekeeper glared at her with angry eyes. 'Whose idea was it?' She turned back to Jamie. 'Yours I expect.

Always gettin' into trouble. I divvent know how your poor mam copes with ya.'

Nisha glanced sideways, her attention sliding from the key to Mrs F and back again. But now that Mrs F had moved, there was no way she could take it without the housekeeper seeing.

Perhaps she would come back later, when Mrs F was busy. Maybe at night.

But the thought of sneaking down to the scullery in the dead of night made her blood run cold. Barrow House was creepy enough in daylight; she couldn't imagine what it would be like skulking about in the suffocating darkness of night.

'Aye, it was me.' Jamie was watching Nisha. 'It was all my doin'. She didn't even knaa I was comin' to the island till I surprised her out on the path.'

'Is that true?' Mrs F raised her eyebrows at Nisha, who shrugged and nodded once.

'Well, I divvent imagine you'll be welcome on the island again,' Mrs Foster said to Jamie. 'Mrs Barrow doesn't like visitors, and this is private property.'

'Aye. I'm sorry.' Jamie lowered his eyes. 'It'll not happen again.'

36

LOOSE LIPS SINK SHIPS

By the time Mrs F had finished cleaning and dressing Jamie's wounds, it was too late for him to go home. The tide was high and there was no way off the island other than the rowing boat.

'But that's for emergencies only,' Mr Foster called from the scullery as he tidied up the bloody mess. 'You'll just have to wait until it gans out again. It'll be clear by six o'clock this evenin'.'

In the kitchen, Mrs F cut two thin slices of cake, put them on to small plates and plonked them down in front of Nisha and Jamie, who were sitting side by side at the table. They each had a cup of weak tea, with a spoonful of sugar to give them energy. Mrs F said they needed it after such a shock.

'I'm not gannin' anywhere.' Jamie dragged his plate towards him as if it was the first time he'd seen food. 'You'd not catch me rowin' out there at high tide. I'd prob'ly drift out to Norway and get sunk by a U-boat.'

'Aye, but your mam'll be beside herself wonderin' where you are,' Mrs F said. 'I knaa I would be.'

Nisha nibbled a corner of cake. It was dry, and not very sweet, but it was better than nothing. Cake was cake. In fact, Nisha was surprised Mrs F had given them any at all. She knew they were lucky to have the eggs, and she'd seen how Mrs F spent ages sieving bran out of the National Flour to make it edible.

Jamie ate his cake in three bites and dabbed up the last crumbs with the tip of his finger. 'Me mam won't miss us,' he said with his mouth full. 'I'm never home before dark, and she'll be busy in the fish shop anyways.' As he spoke, he dropped one hand under the table and tapped Nisha's knee. 'The cake's lovely, by the way. Has it got real eggs in it?'

'Aye, the eggs is real,' Mrs F told him.

'It's delicious,' he said. 'Best I've ever had. You're a canny good cook, Mrs F.'

'Divvent try to charm me, Jamie Harper.' Mrs F hid her smile by turning away and heading to the cold pantry.

As soon as she had her back to them, Jamie tapped

Nisha again. Harder this time.

'What?'

Jamie lightly shook his head, warning her to be quiet, and tapped her again.

When Nisha looked down, Jamie opened his hand to show her what he was holding.

The Master Key.

'Take it,' he whispered.

'I beg your pardon?' Mrs F asked as she returned to the table and laid a few rashers of bacon on the heavy wooden chopping board. 'What did you say?'

'Nowt,' Jamie said as Nisha took the key and slipped it into her pocket. 'I was just sayin' how delicious the cake is.'

Nisha sipped her tea, trying to look innocent.

'Hmm.' Mrs F narrowed her eyes. 'Well, I haven't got time to babysit the pair of you, I've got things to do. And Nisha's mam needs lookin' after. I've been away from her far too long already. See all this fuss you've caused?'

'Ah, they're just young 'uns,' Mr Foster called up from the scullery. 'Everyone's safe and there's nee harm done.' He came to stand at the bottom of the steps and put his muddy boots back on.

'Nee harm done?' Mrs F sliced the bacon harder than she needed to, chopping it into tiny pieces. '*Nee harm done?* I was nearly a widow.'

'It wasn't as bad as all that,' Mr Foster replied.

'And what about poor Mrs Barrow? You think she needs a fright like that? Think of all them memories that must've brought back.'

'Memories?' Nisha put down her cup. 'What kind of memories?'

Mrs F gripped the knife handle so tightly that her knuckles went white. She closed her eyes and took a deep breath. 'Never you mind. Sometimes I talk too much. And loose lips sink ships.' She looked at her husband. 'D'you think she'll be all right?'

'She's in her study with Humphrey.' He stamped his foot into his boot with a *thump-thump-thump*. 'She's got tea and cake and books, so I'd say she'll be canny soon enough.'

'Don't you bang your boots and get mud on my floor,' Mrs F scolded him.

'Not me.' Mr Foster winked at Nisha and Jamie. 'Anyway, I'm off to the garden now, so I'll take these two with me if you like; put 'em to work diggin' and that. I could use the extra hands and it'll keep 'em out of mischief until low tide.'

Nisha could feel the key burning a hole in her pocket. She needed to use it quickly and get it back on the hook before Mrs Foster noticed. 'Can't we just stay indoors?' she asked. 'Please? There are some games in my room – we can play those.'

'What sort of games?' Jamie asked.

'There's something called The Game of Goose that looks a bit boring, but Joy brought Buccaneer,' Nisha said.

'Never heard of it.'

'I can teach you if you like. There's dominoes too.'

Mrs F looked at her husband, who shrugged and said, 'Maybe a bit of quiet is best for 'em.'

'Fine.' Mrs F pointed the knife. There was a tiny strand of bacon fat stuck on the tip. 'But I'll be up to sit with your mam in a minute and I divvent want to hear a sound from either of you. Not a sound, understood? Any trouble and you'll be moppin' the floors for the rest of the week.' She looked at Jamie. '*Both* of you.'

37
BAD THIEF

'How did you do that?' Nisha asked as soon as they were alone in her room.

'Nick the key?' Jamie said. 'Easy. As soon as their backs was turned I just took it. I'm good at stuff like that.'

'And how did you know I wanted it?' She fished the key out of her pocket and turned it around in her fingers. It looked old.

'I could just tell,' he said. 'You'd make a shockin' bad thief. You've got a guilty face.'

Nisha didn't like that word. *Thief.*

'So what's it for anyway?' Jamie asked. 'What's it open?'

Nisha put the key back into her pocket. She didn't really want Jamie to know about the hidden room. Twig had made her promise not to say anything, and she was afraid she might accidentally reveal something if they went to the room together. But she wanted to investigate it as soon as possible, and it would be useful to have Jamie's help.

'A room,' she said. 'At the top of the house. I want to see what's inside.'

'A *secret* room?'

'Well it's not exactly secret but—'

'Are we gannin' there now?'

'Not yet.' Nisha took the Buccaneer game from the drawer and sat cross-legged on the floor. 'Come on, we need to set this up.'

'You can't gan there without me,' Jamie warned. 'That wouldn't be fair. We nicked that key together.'

'I'm not going without you, I need you to keep watch. And anyway, *you* took the key, not *me*.' Nisha hated the idea of stealing. It was wrong. But she had to see what was in that room. Amma and Papa's lives could depend on it.

'But I nicked it for you,' Jamie said. 'That means *we* nicked it.'

'Well, anyway, we didn't *nick* it; we *borrowed* it.' Nisha slipped the game mat from its tube and unrolled it on the floor.

'Aye. "Borrowed". I like that,' Jamie agreed. 'Mind, me

uncle Albert got into bother for "borrowing" his next-door neighbour's wireless one time. Borrowed a pocket watch, too. And twenty-six shillings.'

'It's not the same,' Nisha said. 'We're going to put it back.'

'That's what me uncle Albert said.'

'It's not the same.' Nisha started picking the treasure from the Buccaneer box and placing it on to Treasure Island in the middle of the mat.

'So are we gannin' to find this secret room or not?' Jamie asked. 'This game looks borin'. Sneakin' into a secret room sounds much more fun.'

'We have to wait until Mrs F is in with Amma. My "mam". When she's in there, she won't come out for a while. But if she comes here first, we have to at least look like we're playing this game otherwise she'll know something's up.'

Jamie went to the window and pressed his face close to the glass. 'Well let's hope she doesn't notice the key's gone, else I'll be the one to get wrong for it.'

Nisha put down the game pieces and watched Jamie. She knew what he was looking at. There was a good view of the Weeping Tree from her window.

'I told you not to climb up,' she said.

Jamie didn't answer.

'I told you it was dangerous. You should've done as I said.'

'I never was much good at doin' what I'm told.'

Nisha went to stand beside him. 'I'm sorry.' The shock of it was coming back to her now. She could feel a tremble deep inside her muscles, and there was a tight ache at the back of her neck.

'Sorry for what?' Jamie asked.

'For not helping you.' Nisha felt hot tears suddenly welling in her eyes. She didn't know why they'd started and it made her angry. 'I wanted to help you, I really did, but I just couldn't. It's as if I was stuck.'

'Divvent get all wet on me,' Jamie said. 'I thought you were tough after you nearly died the other day. You didn't blub or nowt.'

Nisha wiped her eyes. 'I'm not tough.'

'Tough*ish*,' Jamie said. 'I mean, you're not tough like a lad – I wouldn't expect you to save me from droppin' off a cliff or nowt like that – but you're not bad for a lass.'

Jamie smiled at her, then they both went to looking out of the window again.

'There's summat queer about that tree,' Jamie said eventually. 'I divvent think it can make wishes come true, but there's definitely summat queer about it.'

'What do you mean?' Nisha asked.

Jamie opened his mouth but hesitated as if he was trying to find the right words and put them in the right order. 'When I fell, summat . . . I divvent knaa.' He shook his head. 'It's stupid.'

'What is?'

Jamie looked down at his hands and stretched out his fingers. 'I thought I was gonna drop right over the crag but summat *grabbed* us. It grabbed us and pulled us closer to the tree. It felt like . . . like a hand grabbin' me wrist. A *cold* hand. It's like the tree saved us.'

Nisha remembered the way Jamie had lurched forward in mid-air.

'And when I went over the edge, summat pushed us against the crag, right on to the tiniest ledge. If I'd missed it . . .' Jamie took a deep breath and let it out. 'I'd be splattered on the rocks or washed out to sea.' He looked at Nisha. 'Either way, I'd be dead.'

Nisha tried not to think about that. The idea of falling and washing out to sea for ever and ever filled her with a most horrifying kind of dread. The kind that eats you up, piece by piece.

38
RETURN TO THE HIDDEN ROOM

It wasn't long before Mrs F came upstairs to find Nisha and Jamie sitting cross-legged on the bedroom floor. A part-played game of Buccaneer was laid out between them.

'I'm off to sit with your mam, now,' Mrs F said. 'I divvent want to hear a sound from you two. Not a peep, remember?'

Nisha and Jamie nodded.

Mrs F glared at them for a moment, but her expression softened as she turned and left them alone.

After that, Nisha and Jamie waited and listened for

what felt like a long time. They didn't dare move until they were sure Mrs F was settled in Amma's room. And even then, they waited a while longer.

Finally, Nisha checked the key was still in her pocket and gave the little red stone a squeeze for luck before she and Jamie crept out into the corridor. It had been Jamie's idea to take off their shoes. He said they'd make less noise that way.

'Be careful where you step,' Nisha told him. 'Everything creaks.'

Jamie pulled a face as if to say he'd done this kind of thing a million times.

Keeping to the carpet that ran along the centre of the passageway, they sneaked towards Amma's room. Nisha expected the door to be shut but, as if to make things difficult for her, Mrs F had left it open. Just halfway, but enough to spot them if they passed by.

She must have done it to keep an eye on them.

'I'll go first.' Jamie started to push past Nisha.

'I should do it,' Nisha said.

'Give over, I thought you wanted us to help. Anyway, I'm better at this than you.'

Nisha couldn't argue with that so she let Jamie lead as they edged closer to the door. She had to admit, he was very good. He hardly made a sound. He even managed to avoid all the creaky floorboards as he leant forward to peer into the room.

'She's sleepin',' he whispered.

Nisha waited as Jamie checked once more, then took a large step across the doorway. He turned and beckoned Nisha.

When Nisha glanced into Amma's room and saw Mrs F asleep in the chair with her knitting in her lap, she felt a sudden wave of guilt. She couldn't shake what Jamie had said – that they had stolen the key. Amma and Papa would have been ashamed of her.

She was a thief.

No; I'm just borrowing the key, she told herself. *And for a good reason.*

She took two quick steps past the doorway and stopped, waiting for any sound from the bedroom.

Nothing.

'Well done,' Jamie said. 'Now where?'

Socks pad-pad-padding on the carpet, they walked quickly and quietly to the end of the passageway and out on to the gallery that overlooked the entrance hall.

Nisha could see straight down to her grandmother's study door. It was firmly shut.

'Which way?' Jamie asked.

Nisha went to the hidden door in the back corner of the gallery. There was no intense cold in the air as there had been when she last went there. No crisp, freezing grip that pinched her skin tight. Instead, there was just the same damp chill that pervaded the rest of the house.

Nisha took a second to wonder if it meant anything, but decided it didn't matter. She had to investigate the room. No matter what.

'What you waitin' for?' Jamie whispered.

'Nothing.' The door creaked when Nisha pulled it open to reveal the twisted staircase. 'Up here.'

They crept upstairs and reached the little landing without incident.

Nisha dug the stolen key from her pocket.

This was the moment of truth. She was beginning to think it would be the wrong key. That somehow the Master Key wouldn't fit this particular lock. And even if the key *did* fit, and the door *did* open, she was afraid of what she might find in there. She remembered the face at the window. Eyes staring from the shadows. Fingers curling around the curtain.

But, worst of all, she was afraid she'd find nothing in there. Nothing that Twig would want.

'Go on, then,' Jamie said. 'Let's get on with it.'

The key did fit.

When Nisha pushed it into the lock, it slid into place without resistance. And when she turned it, there was a solid click as it unlocked.

Nisha took a deep breath and pushed open the door.

39
INSIDE THE HIDDEN ROOM

Nisha had expected it to be musty and old inside the hidden room. She had imagined furniture draped with white sheets, and dust thick enough to write her name in. But the small bedroom was spotless and much cosier than her own. There was no mournful damp like there was in the rest of the house. Here the air smelt of fresh flowers. And even with the curtains drawn across the windows, it was still light enough for it to have a comfortable feel.

There was a fireplace at one end, with a beautiful stone mantelpiece. Carved in the centre of the mantelpiece was a coat of arms, with three words written in a scroll beneath. They were in a language she didn't recognize, so Nisha didn't take much notice of them. She was more interested in the vase of daphnes that stood on top of it. They were just beginning to wilt, but they still smelt sweet.

Against the opposite wall was the head of a large bed that was covered with a dust-free counterpane thrown over the top as if waiting to be turned down later that evening. A golden teddy nestled against the dark wooden headboard.

A bookcase beside the bed was lined with books of all colours and sizes. There were trinkets and knick-knacks on the shelves too. A wind-up monkey. A toy car. A line of lead soldiers. Marbles and jacks. Everything looked dust-free and well-loved, as if their owner would come in at any moment to play with them.

'What are you lookin' for?' Jamie asked.

'I don't know. I just . . . wanted to see.' Nisha went to the wardrobe and opened the door. It stuck a little so she had to give it a tug. The smell of lavender and mothballs wafted out. Inside, a row of dresses waited on hangers. There were three boys' shirts too, and a couple of pairs of shorts. In the bottom of the wardrobe, there was a pair of boots similar to the ones that had belonged to Papa.

'Whose room is this?' Jamie asked. 'Does someone else live in the house? Someone I haven't seen?'

'I . . . I don't know.' Nisha was confused. Everything was so well looked after. Ready to be worn. Ready to be played with. Maybe Jamie was right, maybe someone else *was* living in the house.

All Nisha could do was shake her head and stare at those uncomfortable-looking dresses. They were similar to the one she was wearing right now. Thinking about it made Nisha pull at the neck where it was itching her skin, then she put out a hand and ran her fingers along the dresses and shirts. The hangers creaked as they swung from side to side.

But she wasn't here to look at clothes. She was here to find three lost treasures for Twig. That was all that mattered.

Nisha turned around and scanned the room once more, but nothing jumped out at her. How was she supposed to know what she was looking for?

She felt enormous frustration building inside her. Time was running out and she had no idea what she had to find. She wished she could see Twig again, ask him to tell her, or even just give her a clue.

But maybe it had all been a dream.

'No.' Nisha put her hand to the bracelet to reassure herself. 'It's real.'

'Hm?' Jamie looked at her. 'What did you say?'

'I didn't say anything.' Nisha went to the chest of drawers in the corner and rummaged through, looking for something. Anything. She checked under the bed – completely free of dust – and behind the washstand. She even lifted the rug.

'What are you lookin' for?' Jamie asked. He was inspecting the toys on the bookcase, picking them up one by one to admire them.

'Nothing,' Nisha said.

'Doesn't look like it to me.'

In her frustration, Nisha went to the window. Maybe if she looked out at the tree, Twig would give her a sign. Perhaps whisper the name of what she had to find.

She pulled back the curtain, just a crack, to look out.

The first thing she saw was Humphrey running along the path towards the walled garden. The second thing she saw was her grandmother.

Mrs Barrow was standing on the path looking up at the window. Exactly the way Nisha had been standing when she saw the face earlier that day.

Without thinking, she let go of the curtain and jumped back. 'Oh!'

'What?' Jamie came over. 'What is it?'

'My grandmother. I think she saw me. She's going to kill me.'

'Let's have a look.' Jamie took the corner of the curtain.

'Don't!' Nisha warned him.

'I'll be careful.' He crouched down and lifted the

curtain the tiniest amount. He put his eyes closer and peered out. 'Neebody there,' he said.

Nisha's insides churned. 'She's coming.'

'What?'

'She must have seen me and now she's coming up here,' Nisha said. 'Quick, we have to get out!' She pulled Jamie to his feet and shoved him towards the door. 'Go!'

Nisha was frantic. They had to get down the stairs and across the gallery before her grandmother came inside.

'Hurry!' She pulled Jamie to the door, shoved him out on to the landing, and grabbed the door handle to pull it shut. As she did so, she took one last look around the room to make sure everything was exactly as they had found it.

The wardrobe door was open. Just a crack.

She ran back into the bedroom and pushed the wardrobe door shut. That's when she noticed the curtain wasn't straight.

'Howay!' Jamie hissed as Nisha smoothed out the curtain.

But as Nisha scanned the room one last time, she realized something wasn't right. Something was different.

But what was it? Was it something important?

Her gaze was drawn to the lead soldiers on the bookcase and she knew what it was.

'Give it back.' Nisha held out her hand. 'Give me the soldier.'

'What?' Jamie tried to look innocent.

Downstairs, the front door creaked open.

'You know exactly what. Come on, we haven't got time for this.'

Jamie sighed and took the soldier from the pocket of his shorts. 'Neebody would miss it.'

'Someone would.' Nisha snatched it from his hand. 'Someone kept this room in perfect order – they would definitely notice if something was missing.'

She hurried over to the bookcase and returned the soldier to his rightful place.

As they hurried downstairs, they heard Mrs Barrow's clickety-clack heels on the stones in the hallway below. She was moving quickly.

Nisha and Jamie ran as fast as they dared. They raced down to the main gallery and eased the hidden door shut before ducking low and hurrying across the landing. They made it to the bedroom passageway just as Nisha's grandmother reached the top of the stairs. If she had looked to her right, she would have seen them disappearing around the corner—

—and bumping right into Mrs F.

'What are you two up to?' Mrs F eyed them with suspicion.

'Nothing,' Nisha said, thinking quickly. 'Just playing hide and seek.'

'Hide an' seek? You're supposed to be in your room, playin' board games.'

'Aye,' Jamie said. 'But we got bored of that. An' we were bein' quiet. You didn't hear a peep from us, did you?' He gave Mrs F his best smile.

Mrs F studied them long and hard, then tightened her lips.

'Hmm,' she said finally. 'Well. I'm just poppin' down to the kitchen but I'll be back in a tick.' She looked at Jamie. 'Stay out of trouble.'

'Blimey, that was close,' Jamie said as they put the Buccaneer pieces back in the box.

'You tried to steal that lead soldier.' Nisha didn't even try to hide her anger.

'Borrow,' Jamie said. 'Like with the key.'

'I'm going to put the key back,' Nisha said. 'As soon as we go downstairs. I told you that.' She jammed the lid back on the box, squashing one corner. 'Don't be like your uncle Albert.'

Jamie frowned and lowered his eyes. 'Sorry.'

But Nisha didn't get the chance to put the key back, because when they went down to the kitchen, Mrs F was still there, and she was angrier than Nisha had ever seen her.

In fact, she was *livid*.

Because she had already noticed the key was missing.

40

CAUGHT

'Get in 'ere!' Mrs F grabbed Jamie as soon as he stepped into the kitchen. She pulled him past the table towards the scullery.

'Ow!' Jamie tried to escape. 'Get off me!' But Mrs F gripped him like a vice.

Nisha followed as the housekeeper dragged him down the steps and stood him in front of the rack of hooks.

Just like before, there were keys and a dog lead and a rusty chain hanging from the hooks, but one of them was empty.

'What have you got to say for yoursel', you thievin' little gypsy?' Her whole face was the colour of beetroot.

'I—' Jamie opened his mouth, but Mrs F slapped him on the back of the head with a solid *whack!*

It was the sound of Dewi hitting dust out of a mat. The sound of Mr Hill's belt.

'Be sure you divvent lie to me,' said Mrs F.

Jamie rubbed his head. 'Ow! What?' he said. 'I done nowt. I—'

Mrs F grabbed the scruff of his neck and made him look at the empty hook.

'Don't lie to me,' she warned him.

'Oh,' he said.

'"Oh", indeed!' Mrs F gave him another whack. 'I shoulda known you'd be a little thief.' She turned him around and gave him a shake just as Mr Foster came in from outside.

'What's gannin' on?' he asked.

'We have a thief in the house.' Mrs F explained what had happened.

Mr Foster didn't seem quite so bothered as his wife. He just took off his cap and shook his head at Jamie. 'Your fatha would be ashamed o' you,' he said.

Nisha couldn't bear it. Jamie was saying nothing about why he had taken the key. Mr and Mrs Foster thought he was guilty just because of who he was. The same way everyone believed Nisha when she had told them that David Hill threw the stone. Because he was the sort of boy who would.

But Jamie had stolen the key for *her*. It was *her* fault as much as his.

On the other hand, Mrs F was in such a rage, it frightened Nisha almost to death. She had never seen someone so angry before, and she didn't want Mrs F to whack her head the way she kept whacking Jamie's. She could just stay quiet and let Jamie take the blame. It would be easier.

Let someone else take all the blame.

'Where is it?' Mrs F was saying. 'Where did you put it, you little thief?' She whacked him again and reached down to check Jamie's pockets. 'Plannin' on sellin' it on to some other good-for-nowt thieves, were you? Just you wait till your mam hears about this. She'll take a belt and bray you within an inch of your miserable little thievin' life.'

A belt.

Nisha remembered David Hill, dragged away from the convoy to feel the lick of his father's belt. Punished for a crime he didn't commit. The guilt of it surfaced like poison in her heart. It was too late to say sorry to David Hill, but it wasn't too late to save Jamie's skin. The boy who had once saved her life.

So Nisha plucked up the courage to step forward.

'Stop!' she said. 'Leave him alone! I . . . I have it.' She took the key from her pocket and held it up. 'It's here.'

Mrs F looked back at Nisha. Mr Foster frowned as if

he were trying to work out what was going on.

'So he gave it to you to look after, did he?' Mrs F said finally. 'Make you a . . . a what-do-you-call-it? A . . . a . . .'

'Accomplice,' Nisha said.

'Aye, that's it. An *accomplice*.'

Nisha shook her head. 'I took it. It was me.'

Mrs F stopped. Her whole face fell. 'You? *You* took it?'

Nisha held the key out towards Mrs F. 'I'm sorry. It wasn't his fault. Jamie didn't do it. I did.'

Mrs F took the key and narrowed her eyes. 'You're not just sayin' that to stop him gettin' into trouble?'

Nisha shook her head.

'Why did you take it?' Mr Foster asked.

'I wanted to see inside the hidden room,' Nisha said. 'At the top of the house.'

'That's out of bounds,' said Mrs F. 'No one's allowed up there.'

'I'm sorry,' Nisha said again. She wanted to ask who the room belonged to, but she had a feeling this wouldn't be the best time. And anyway, she was beginning to wonder if she might already know.

Extract from Nisha Barrow's Truth, 1942

There's a swimming pool near the tennis courts at the club on the plantation. If it hasn't been bombed. Amma and Papa used to play tennis with the Youngs and the Knudsens and I would run across the sharp grass and jump into the water. It was always cool after being in the sun. Sometimes there were other children there but I liked it most when I had the pool to myself. I used to sink down and sit on the bottom. It's hard to stay down when you're full of air, because you keep floating up, so I'd have to let my breath out in a trickle of bubbles. The best thing was to close my eyes, hold my nose and see how long I could last. Underwater, everything is different. Like it's the real world but not quite the real world.

After the attack on the convoy, I felt like I was underwater because everything was not quite real. Papa shook me and I looked up to see him sitting beside me with his face all dirty. There was blood on him, but not his. Amma was there too, with her beautiful hair all full of dirt and leaves and sewage. Her sari was torn even more.

We climbed out of the ditch and stood on the road but it wasn't really a road any more. The cars at the front of the convoy were all right - including ours -

but everything further back was smashed to bits. The road was full of holes and there were burning cars scattered all over the place. Black smoke was pouring into the air. There were broken trees and leaves and branches everywhere too. Orange fire pushed the night back into the jungle.

My hair was wet for some reason. It was sticking to my face and I think it might have been sweat because of the heat from the fires. The sleeve of my dress was singed and there was a small burn on my arm. I was only wearing one sandal. I don't know what happened to the other one.

People wandered about among the fires, crying and screaming and moaning. Some people just stood there like they had nothing inside them. Others were searching for people. Calling out their names.

Worst of all, one of the bombs had hit the drainage ditch on our side of the road but further up. It was nothing but a massive crater. David Hill was sitting beside the burning hole with dirt and blood on him. He was looking about and blinking like he didn't know where he was. Right next to him was his amma and what was left of his papa.

I couldn't stop staring at David Hill just sitting there looking confused. Even when Amma tried to drag me away, I couldn't move. Papa had to pick me up and put me in the back of the car. He kept whispering to me, telling me to be brave. But I didn't feel brave, I felt terrible. The whole world was collapsing in on me. Crushing me and turning black.

When Papa started the engine and drove away, David Hill was on his feet. Someone was helping him and his amma into a truck, just leaving his papa lying dead on the road.

And I didn't get the chance to own up to what I did.

41

FRIENDS

Mrs F didn't tell Nisha off the way she had Jamie. Nisha thought it was a bit unfair but she didn't complain.

'She's scary when she's cross,' Jamie said as they walked down towards the causeway. 'Even worse than me mam.' They stopped when they reached the stone pathway across the sand. 'Thanks for ownin' up, though,' he said.

'I'm sorry I didn't own up sooner,' Nisha said. 'I shouldn't have let her hit you like that. Not even once.'

'It's nee botha really. I would've taken any punishment. For you, I'd have taken it. I would.'

Nisha didn't know what to say to that. She'd never

had a friend like Jamie before.

Jamie kicked the toe of his boot into the wet sand and looked across at the mainland. 'I asked for me da' to be alive,' he said.

'What?' Nisha turned her head to hear him properly.

'At the tree. That's what I wished for.' Jamie lifted his eyes to the grey sky. His words sounded tight in his throat. 'I wished for me da' to be alive. Yours too.'

'Mine?'

'Aye, but it doesn't work, does it? The tree, I mean? And even if it does, it can't bring back the dead, eh?' Jamie took a deep breath and blinked away his tears. 'I'm not cryin',' he said.

'I know.' Nisha slipped her hand into her pocket and squeezed the red stone. 'I'm sorry I didn't help you when you fell. I couldn't move. I was so scared.'

'We all get scared sometimes,' Jamie said.

'Not you though. I don't think you're scared of anything.'

'I divvent knaa.' He glanced back towards the house. 'I'm scared of that Mrs F. The way she clipped me round the heed.' When he smirked, a small tear fell from the corner of his eye. He wiped it away with his hand. 'Well. Best be off. See you on the morrow maybe?'

'Maybe.'

'Thanks again,' he said. 'For ownin' up.'

*

Nisha stayed on the beach, watching Jamie follow the causeway path back to the mainland. When he was halfway across, just a small streak of colour near the stilted hut, he turned and waved.

Nisha raised a hand to wave back, and felt something warm on her wrist. It was as if a ring of sunshine had lit up beneath her coat sleeve.

The bracelet.

She lowered her arm and pushed up her coat sleeve. The bracelet was still there, the same dark wood, the same tightness around her wrist. But something was different. Between two of the lines, there was now a word. Carved in beautiful scripted handwriting, it glowed like liquid gold. Nisha turned it from side to side, letting it catch the grey light as she tried to make out what it said. Just one word. But although it looked a bit like English, it wasn't a word she'd ever heard before.

honestas.

42

HONESTAS

The word spun around her head as she made her way back to Barrow House.

honestas.

What on earth could it mean?

One thing was for sure – it was important. The bracelet had grown warm around her wrist, and the word was still glowing in the wood as if it had been burnt there. She began to think it was a clue telling her what she had to find. If she could work out what it meant, it might lead her to the right place. Nisha almost tripped several times on the way up to the house because she didn't dare take her eyes off it.

When she pushed through the front door, Grandmother was waiting in the hallway. She was standing straight as a broom, with Humphrey sitting at her heel. As soon as Nisha saw her, everything came flooding back and she was sure she was going to get into trouble for what happened on the crag. She shouldn't have been near the Weeping Tree – it was one of the rules, and she had been told *so many* times. Her grandmother was certain to be angry about it, and about Jamie being on the island without her knowing.

Nisha also wondered if Mrs F had told her grandmother about the stolen key.

Humphrey came running over the moment Nisha walked through the door. He jumped up and put his paws on her legs, then ran around her feet, wondering why she wasn't tickling him. Nisha was surprised her grandmother didn't order him back to heel.

'Is your friend all right?' Mrs Barrow asked. 'He gave us all quite a shock.'

Nisha nodded and lowered her eyes. 'I'm sorry about what happened.'

'Not half as sorry as he was, I expect.' Mrs Barrow shuddered. 'He's lucky to be alive.'

Surprised by her soft tone, Nisha looked up to see that her grandmother's eyes were red. The skin beneath her eyelids was puffy.

'Please,' Mrs Barrow said. 'Don't go there again. Will

you promise not to go to the tree again? It is such a dangerous place. I won't ban you from the flower garden, or anywhere else on the island. I don't even mind if your friend comes here, but please stay away from that tree.'

Nisha nodded.

'Let me hear you say it.'

'I promise,' Nisha said.

Humphrey banged his tail against her shins, so Nisha crouched to stroke his head. The prospect of attention made Humphrey's excitement levels go sky-high. His bottom was wagging at one hundred miles per hour.

'I really *am* sorry,' Nisha said. 'I don't mean to be any trouble.'

Mrs Barrow gave Nisha a tight-lipped smile. If anything, she seemed sad rather than angry.

'Is everything all right?' Nisha asked. 'I mean, apart from what happened?'

'Yes.' Mrs Barrow put a hand to her mouth for a moment before taking it away.

'Still no word from Papa?' Nisha asked.

Mrs Barrow shook her head. 'Still no word, I'm afraid. But I'm sure there'll be news soon. We must have hope.'

Upstairs, there was no change with Amma. She was still lying feverish in bed. Mrs F was watching over her, sitting in the armchair with her knitting. Nisha stood quietly in the cold passageway, looking through the crack in the open bedroom door because she didn't want to face Mrs F; she was still scared and embarrassed about what had happened with Jamie and the key.

But it wasn't long before the housekeeper glanced up and spotted her.

'Don't stand there like a ghost,' she said. 'Come in.' Mrs F didn't sound angry.

Nisha slipped over to the bed and put her hands in her pockets, looking down at Amma. It had only been a few days but she'd already lost a lot of weight. Her face was drawn tight around her cheekbones. Her lips were thin and her skin was drained of colour.

'She's had some water,' Mrs F said. 'And I managed to get some soup in her.'

Amma opened her eyes just a crack.

'Amma?' Nisha felt a trickle of hope. 'Are you awake?'

Amma slowly lifted one hand to beckon her. When Nisha leant down, Amma put her hand on Nisha's head and pulled her close so they were cheek to cheek.

'My baby,' she whispered, then closed her eyes.

Nisha sat there for a while, but that was the only thing Amma said.

'It's not been a good day, has it?' Mrs F said quietly. 'First the tree and then the key.' She put down her knitting and sighed. 'You're a good lass, Nisha, I know you are. You're just a bairn and you got curious, so let this be the end of it. It's time to start respectin' your grandmother's wishes. And no more stealin'.'

Stealing. Such a harsh and heavy word. It made Nisha cringe just at the thought of how much one word can mean.

And like that, another word leapt into her head.

honestas.

She felt the warmth of the bracelet around her wrist.

honestas. What did it mean? Perhaps the answer was somewhere in the hidden room.

When Joy came up from the village that evening, they played a game of Buccaneer in Amma's room. The map was spread out on the floor and they sat opposite each other with the pieces all laid out, but Nisha's heart just wasn't in it.

'What's the matter?' Joy asked as she took another of Nisha's treasures. 'Something's on your mind. Something more than usual, I mean.'

She was right about that. There were a *lot* of things on Nisha's mind.

Nisha sighed. She was afraid to ask, in case it broke her agreement with Twig, but . . . 'Do you know what "honestas" is?'

'"Honestas"?' Joy frowned. '"Honestas". Is it French? It sounds familiar. Like the word "honest". I've heard it before somewhere.'

'Really?' Nisha perked up. 'Where?'

Joy scrunched up her face as she tried to remember.

Nisha hung on, holding her breath, but eventually Joy just shook her head.

'It's right there,' she said. 'On the tip of my tongue. Well, not on the tip of my tongue, but right there at the front of my head and – no, sorry. I can't get it.'

Nisha sighed with disappointment.

'Don't worry,' Joy said. 'It'll come to me.'

43

THE FIRST LOST
TREASURE

That night, the Weeping Tree called to her again.

Nisha was huddled beneath the blankets, curled into a ball as thoughts tumbled through her head. Thoughts about Amma and Papa, and about Jamie's brush with death, and how something had saved him from falling. Despite what everyone said about him, and despite the fact that he'd tried to steal the lead soldier, Nisha liked Jamie. There was something wild about him, that was for sure, but she knew he would always be a fiercely loyal friend.

She also thought about the sadness she had seen in her

grandmother's eyes that evening. It seemed to Nisha that there was an awful *lot* of sadness in Barrow House, and that they could do with more people like Joy and Jamie to brighten it up. Mrs F did her best, but she must have been here so long the grey, cold house had worked its way into her bones.

Most of all, though, Nisha thought about the strange word that had appeared on the bracelet.

honestas.

She looked at it, glowing like fire, and traced the tip of her finger around it until she fell asleep with the sound of it swimming in her head.

And then the tree called to her.

Like before, Nisha woke to find herself on the overgrown path. The wind was high, blustering about her, plucking at the coat she didn't remember putting on. Once again, she was barefoot, but her feet weren't cold, and she hardly noticed the damp grass blowing against her ankles.

The clouds were a fine veil of silk across the sky, and the almost-full moon was a single watchful eye looking through it. Silvery light shimmered on the waves, so that from the path it appeared as if tears were weeping from the branches of the tree standing guard on the crag.

The wind called again and Nisha saw the figure standing beneath the tree.

Twig.

As soon as she laid eyes on him, he slipped away out of sight.

Nisha had promised Mrs F that she wouldn't go near the tree again. She had promised her grandmother the same thing, and Nisha was not one to break her promises.

But maybe there were times when promises had to be broken.

Amma and Papa's lives might depend on a broken promise.

Without fear, she glided along the path. Her feet hardly seemed to touch the ground. If there were jagged stones in the dirt, she didn't feel them. And when she came close, she was not afraid of the crag.

That afternoon, in the stark grey light of day, she had been terrified of approaching the edge. Her fear had fixed her to the spot like it was alive inside her, but now? Now she felt nothing but peace as she stepped from root to root, reaching for the first branches and climbing as if they were steps built just for her. The tree shifted and twisted to accommodate her. When she needed a branch to hold on to, one appeared. When she needed a foothold, one grew beneath her.

The trapdoor was open – of course it was – and Nisha had no trouble climbing up into the tree house. She went to the window and looked out across the sea.

'You found something.'

Nisha turned around to see Twig standing in the shadows. She could just make out his shape.

He stepped forward and held out his hand. 'May I see?'

Nisha raised her arm and the sleeve of her nightdress slipped back to reveal the bracelet around her wrist. The word carved into it was like a curling river of fire that flickered in Twig's eyes.

He took Nisha's hand.

His skin was cold.

'What does it mean?' Nisha asked.

Twig smiled a faraway smile. It played on his lips and glittered in his eyes.

'It means you have found the first of three. You found Honesty.' His mouth hardly moved when he spoke.

'Honesty?' Nisha asked. 'I found honesty? But I don't understand.'

'You told the truth when you could have lied.'

'About the key?' Nisha asked. 'Is that it? It's because I told them about the key? Because I told them it wasn't Jamie, that it was all my fault?'

'And now I need you to find two more treasures. But time is running out, and I can't help you without all three.'

'Why not?'

'Because that's how it is.'

'So what *are* they?' Nisha asked. 'What *are* the other two things? Please tell me.'

Twig shook his head. 'You have to find them for yourself. Only you can—'

The air grew colder and the wind picked up. The Weeping Tree moaned as if something ached deep in its roots. Its branches swayed, and the tree house moved like a ship rolling on the heartless expanse of the grey North Sea.

'What's happening?' Nisha steadied herself.

'Something's coming,' Twig said. 'Something terrible. You have to stop it. You have to help.'

'What is it?' Nisha went to the window and looked through the branches at the shape of Barrow House. 'What's coming?'

'Danger,' Twig said.

'What kind of danger?' Nisha felt her tension rising. *What's coming?*

But Twig reached out and took her hand, and Nisha felt a drowsy warmth flood through her. Then she was slipping away as sleepiness overcame her.

'Help me,' Twig said. 'Help me.'

FULL MOON

44
DANGER

Late the following afternoon, Mr Foster strode into the flower garden holding an axe.

Nisha was sitting on Elizabeth's bench with her journal on her lap. The sky was heavy with cloud, as usual, and the air was cold.

Nisha stopped writing and looked up when Mr Foster appeared.

She had woken that morning with an awful sense of dread. It stayed with her every moment, digging deeper and deeper into her thoughts.

Twig had warned her that something terrible was going to happen, and when she saw Mr Foster carrying his axe, she knew what it was.

At first, she was too afraid to say anything. Too afraid to know.

She watched Mr Foster stride along the path towards the far corner of the garden. His boots clumped on the stones.

When he lifted the curtain of ivy and disappeared, the spell broke and Nisha jumped to her feet.

'Mr Foster!'

She tucked the notebook and pencil into her pocket and ran after him.

By the time she slipped through the curtain, Mr Foster was halfway along the overgrown path.

'Mr Foster!'

He stopped and turned.

There was a menacing look to him, standing there silhouetted against the sky and the sea. The axe hung from his right hand. The Weeping Tree clawed its way from the ground behind him.

'What are you doing?' Her words were breathless as she ran towards him. The air was cold in her lungs. 'Where are you going with that axe?'

She already knew the answer. There was only one place he could be going. Only one thing he could be doing.

'Mrs Barrow wants it down,' he said when Nisha reached him.

'You can't.' Nisha could hardly get the words out. 'You can't kill it.'

'Kill it?' Mr Foster looked puzzled.

'You can't cut it down.'

'It's what Mrs Barrow wants.'

'But it's – it's too important.'

Mr Foster adjusted his cap and frowned. 'Important how?'

Nisha closed her eyes and tried to control her emotions. There was so much fear and frustration. There was so much at stake. If Twig was the heart of the tree, then how would he live if the tree was cut down? And if Twig was gone, what would happen to Amma and Papa? This was what he had meant when he said that danger was coming. Somehow, he had known that Mr Foster would be bringing his axe.

'Please,' Nisha begged. 'Just – please. Don't hurt the tree.'

Mr Foster's shoulders slumped. 'Look, pet, it's probably for the best. If you knew the things that have happened here. That lad yesterday was the least of it.'

'But we'll stay away from it.' Urgency and desperation were starting to overwhelm her. 'I promise.'

'Aye, well, that young lad is lucky to be alive. And now Mrs B is worried. It mightn't always look like it, but she's concerned about you. She doesn't want nowt to happen to you.'

'I'll keep away.' Nisha tightened her hands into fists. 'I *promise*.' She wanted to tell him why the tree was so important. If she told him, he wouldn't cut it down. But she'd promised Twig she wouldn't tell a soul.

'Just – please.' Her throat tightened and her eyes stung. Without thinking, she reached out and tried to take the axe from Mr Foster's hand, but he pulled it away and stepped back.

'I'm sorry, pet. It's what she wants.'

'Then I'll get her to change her mind.'

'How you gonna dee that?'

'I'll talk to her. Just don't do anything yet. *Please*.'

Mr Foster looked at his axe, then at Nisha. 'Sorry, pet. It's me job to dee what Mrs B wants. And I think she's right. I should've done this a long time ago.'

'No. I'll make her keep the tree. I'll *make* her.' With tears filling her eyes, Nisha turned and ran back along the path. She would go to the house and do whatever it took to make her grandmother save the Weeping Tree. Amma and Papa's lives depended on it.

'You'll have a job on your hands,' Mr Foster called after her.

Nisha stopped and looked back. 'What?'

'Mrs Barrow's gone to the mainland. Took the pony and trap. I'm sorry, pet.'

With that, Mr Foster hefted the axe in his right hand, turned, and headed out to the Weeping Tree.

45

A BROKEN PROMISE

The wind gathered across the island as Nisha sprinted through the garden towards the house. When she emerged from the protection of the walls, it struck her like a fist, buffeting her as she hurried along the path. She put her head down and pushed through it. She had to get to the mainland as fast as she could. The only way to save the tree was to persuade her grandmother to let it stand.

As she ran, her breath came in short, sharp gasps. The cold air stung her throat and lungs. It brought memories of seawater flooding into her. Of the sherbet lemon – something so simple and so sweet – catching in her windpipe and almost stealing her life. Her thoughts were a panicked jumble of how she might persuade her grandmother to save the Weeping Tree.

Nisha pushed herself as hard as she could, running up the path, and around to the back of the house. Chickens scattered in all directions as she rushed across the courtyard, grabbed Papa's bike, and pushed it out on to the path.

Nisha flew with the wind at her back, pedalling hard and fast.

She reached the dunes, embraced by the long grass, and then she was whizzing out on to the causeway. The tyres slipped on the slick stones and strands of seaweed that lay across them. Water sprayed up around her. It was terrifying and exhilarating all at once, but Nisha kept the bicycle straight, and focused her mind. She had to save the tree.

Save the tree; save Twig.

Save Twig; save Amma and Papa.

For ever and ever, Nisha was in that dangerous no man's land of sand and stone. She flew across with nothing but the wind in her ear and the *shhhhhhh* of the bicycle tyres on the wet causeway. She pedalled harder and harder, never daring to slow down, not even for a second, before finally she bumped on to the dunes at the other side and climbed towards the village.

*

The first people she saw were a group of young women wearing green and brown. They were on the pavement, heading towards the shops, giggling and joking. Nisha could hear their voices, even with her bad ears, so they must have been loud.

Their uniform made them look like they were all the same person, but when they stopped, laughing at some joke or another, Nisha spotted a blaze of red hair, and knew at once who it was.

'Joy!' She screeched to a halt beside them. 'Joy!'

Joy came over to the edge of the pavement. 'What is it? Is something wrong? Is it your mam?'

'Have you seen my grandmother?' Nisha was so out of breath, she could hardly get the words out.

'Mrs Barrow?'

'Yes. She's driving the pony and trap.'

'Oh.' Joy's eyes lit up. 'Aye. She was going that way.' She pointed along the street, further into the village. 'What's the matter? Is everything all right?'

Nisha looked the way Joy had pointed, hoping to catch a glimpse of the pony and trap, but instead she saw Jamie jogging towards her.

'What's gannin' on?' he asked.

By now the other land girls were starting to gather round. There were some children on the green too, who had stopped and were wandering over.

'I'm looking for my grandmother,' Nisha said. 'It's important.'

'I saw her headin' up to the church,' Jamie said. 'It's just outside the village. Howay, give us a backie and I'll show you.' Without waiting for an answer, he jumped on the back of her bicycle and grabbed hold of her ribs. 'Let's gan.'

Leaving Joy and her friends at the side of the road, Nisha pushed down hard on the pedals and set off.

'Be careful!' Joy called after them.

It was difficult at first, riding with Jamie on the back, but he let his legs hang either side to help keep balance, and soon they picked up speed.

'Just keep gannin' this way!' Jamie shouted in her ear. 'Follow the road until I tell ya!'

Nisha sped out of the village. Hedges and fields flashed past, and when Jamie finally directed her off the main road on to a narrow lane, Nisha saw the church spire through the trees.

They found Bonny standing at the church gate. The trap was still hitched to her, and she had her head down, cropping the grass that grew at the foot of the low stone wall.

'She must be inside,' Jamie said as Nisha brought the bicycle to a stop. 'What's this all about?' He jumped off. 'What's gannin' on?'

Nisha didn't reply. She let the bicycle fall against the wall and hurried through the gate into the churchyard.

Jamie followed.

Mrs Barrow wasn't in the church. She was in the graveyard.

Nisha spotted her straight away, standing at the far end wearing a heavy coat and a hat. She was straight-backed but with her head bowed, and looked as if she might have been there a long time. Almost as if she were a statue.

Nisha stopped running.

'Wait here,' she said to Jamie, then made her way among the headstones towards her grandmother.

Most of the gravestones were old. *Old* old. They were covered in moss or so badly eroded by the sea air that the names were hardly legible any more. One or two were a little newer, the grey stone still free of moss as if relatives came from time to time to tidy them up and remember their lost loved ones.

'Nisha.' Mrs Barrow looked up when she heard footsteps. 'What . . . Is everything all right? You look flustered.'

Nisha quickly smoothed down her coat and stood up straighter. She brushed the hair from her face and tried to catch her breath. Her chest was still heaving from the effort of cycling all the way from Barrow Island.

'Is something the matter?' Mrs Barrow took a step forward. She reached out as if she were going to touch Nisha's face, then stopped. Her hand hung in mid-air for a moment before she lowered it.

'Don't kill it,' Nisha managed to blurt out between breaths. 'Please don't kill it.'

'What on earth are you . . .? Oh.' Mrs Barrow's face fell. 'The tree.'

Nisha nodded and came closer. 'Please don't cut it down. Please.'

'I'm afraid it's too late for that,' said Mrs Barrow. 'I've asked Mr Foster to see to it. I expect he'll be cutting it as we speak.'

'You can't let him. It's too—'

'It's for the best,' Mrs Barrow said. 'I should have cut it down years ago.'

'But it's too important.' Nisha reached out to take her grandmother's gloved hand. 'I need that tree.'

Mrs Barrow looked at Nisha's small hand holding hers. 'Why? Whatever do you mean?'

'I need it. If you kill it, you'll kill Twig—' A jolt of horror shook her. Nisha couldn't believe she'd said his name out loud. She wasn't supposed to. She had broken the agreement.

'What did you say?' Mrs Barrow pulled her hand from Nisha's and stepped back.

But all Nisha could do was shake her head with regret

and dismay. She had already said too much. She had promised she wouldn't say anything about Twig. Now she had a sudden feeling of sinking in wet sand. As if something was dragging her down and suffocating her. She should never have said anything. She should never have said his name. Twig would know. He would refuse to help her.

'What did you say?' Mrs Barrow asked again. She frowned as if she was puzzling over something.

But Nisha continued to shake her head. 'Please. You have to save the tree.'

Mrs Barrow set her jaw tight and stared.

Nisha thought she was in trouble now. For disturbing her grandmother in the churchyard. For being disrespectful. For being from another country, and because her father had married an Indian instead of a nice English girl. Mrs Barrow was going to let out all her hatred for Nisha.

But instead, there was a change in Mrs Barrow's expression like there had been that day in her study. Her frown softened and her jaw relaxed. It was as if a blurred memory was coming into focus. She crouched down to take Nisha's hands and look into her eyes. 'That tree is really important to you, isn't it?'

'Yes.'

Mrs Barrow's own eyes suddenly twinkled as if she had found some treasure that had been lost for a long time. 'Goodness. I think it's important to me too.'

Nisha didn't know what to say. She was surprised by the sudden change, but was glad to see it.

'Yes.' Mrs Barrow stood up as if she were waking from a dream. 'It *is* important. You're quite right. Come along, then,' she said. 'Let's go and save that tree.'

She set off through the churchyard, pulling Nisha by the hand.

As they turned away, Nisha caught a glimpse of the well-kept grave Mrs Barrow had been visiting.

The dark headstone looked almost as if it were new. There was no moss growing on it, and there were only a few signs of wear and tear. Carefully placed beneath it was a bunch of daphnes. But, most of all, it was the name that caught Nisha's eye.

Elizabeth Barrow.

After the attack on the convoy, Papa drove all the way through the night without stopping. I pretended to be asleep on the back seat because I didn't want to talk to anyone about anything. All I could think about was David Hill sitting on the road beside his dead papa.

When we arrived at the docks in Singapore early the next morning, I felt numb. As if someone had torn everything out of me. So many awful things had happened and it was never going to end. The awful things were just going to go on and on.

The docks were in chaos. It was like the Thursday market times one thousand. Already there were cars and trucks and carts and motorbikes and bicycles and people and soldiers everywhere. There was so much noise and smell and shouting and crying.

We didn't stop to take our things out of the boot, we just left the car where we stopped. Nobody cared about their cars any more. Some people even pushed them right off the dock into the sea to stop the Japanese from having them.

Amma held my hand in one of hers. In the other she held Papa's as he dragged us among the abandoned cars and through the frightened crowds. We were dirty and burnt and I only had one sandal but I hardly even noticed because there were people all round us like a sea of fear and I was scared I would get lost, or forgotten. I kept hearing people say things like:

'... the Japanese have taken Penang ...'

'... they're coming through the jungle on bicycles ...'

'... it's only a matter of days before Singapore falls ...'

We held on to each other as we pushed through the crowd. Papa told us that a chap he used to be at school with was in charge of boarding. He said, 'He'll get you on.' There was something I didn't like about the way he said it but I didn't know what it was.

When I saw the ship, I couldn't believe how big it was. It was painted black, with three funnels. Hundreds of people were on deck, pressed against the sides, waving to others waiting on the dock below. Near the front of the ship, 'Empress of India' was painted in massive white letters. I thought that it was funny (funny strange, I mean) that we were going to escape on the Empress of India, because Amma is from India, and I'm half Indian.

There was a big noisy crowd near the bottom of the steps that led up to the gangplank. People were getting angry, waving papers, shoving others out of the way. A group of soldiers was pushing them back, while an officer in uniform stood ticking people's names off a list. As we got closer and Papa started talking to him, I heard something that made me so scared. One of the soldiers pushing against the crowd shouted, 'Get back! Women and children only. And if your name's not on the list, you have to wait.'

Women and children only. That's when I understood why I didn't like what Papa had said earlier. He had said, 'He'll get _you_ on.' Not, 'He'll get _us_ on.' And then I had the most awful feeling in my heart because I realized that Papa wasn't going on the ship with us. My whole chest filled up like I was drowning and I wanted to tell him that he had to come with us. Or that if he was staying in Singapore, we would stay with him. But before I could say anything, we heard planes coming again and the air raid sirens started up all around the docks. The pushing and shouting got worse then, because people were going in all directions. A few seconds later, the first Japanese planes came out of the sky, firing machine guns at the crowd. How could they? People were just trying to be safe, trying to keep their children and wives and husbands safe. But then there was blood and they were all dying and screaming and falling over. It was the most horrible thing imaginable and I wanted to close my eyes and wish it all away but suddenly I saw David Hill just a few feet away. The crowd parted at exactly the right time and there he was standing on the docks with his amma. Just standing there. And I suddenly knew that I had to say sorry for what I had done and for what had happened to him. I had to tell his amma that it was me who threw the stone. It felt like it was the most important thing in the world. The last thing David and his amma would remember about Mr Hill was him taking off his belt and beating David for something he didn't even do. Something that was my fault and I could never change but I had to say sorry, I had to. So I let go of Amma's hand and stepped towards him and then the bomb hit us.

46

WE'LL NEVER MAKE IT

Mrs Barrow ushered Nisha on to the trap without a word, then climbed up beside her and took the reins.

'The bicycle —' Nisha looked back.

'I'll follow you.' Jamie jumped on the bicycle and waited for Mrs Barrow to crack her whip in the air over Bonny's head and drive back towards the village.

As they came out of the lane and turned on to the main road, they saw Joy striding towards them, but Mrs Barrow didn't slow down.

'Is everything all right?' Joy shouted. 'Do you need help?'

'Can't stop!' Nisha replied. 'Sorry! I'll see you later!'

And then they turned a bend in the road and left Joy behind.

The trap jostled and jumped with every bump and hole in the road, but Nisha hardly even noticed. She was thrilled that her grandmother had changed her mind about the Weeping Tree. Something Nisha said had lit a fire in Mrs Barrow's eyes, and now she was acting as if nothing was going to stop her from getting to Barrow Island to halt Mr Foster's axe.

But the broken promise. The dark thought crept into Nisha's head. *You said his name. You broke your promise.*

They raced through the village with Jamie pedalling behind them like mad.

Bonny kept up her pace, trotting past the shops and down the road towards the causeway. She moved with her ears pricked up and her head high, as if she knew she was on an important mission.

When they reached the causeway, though, Nisha's heart sank.

'Oh my goodness,' Mrs Barrow said. 'I must have lost track of time at the churchyard. Look at the tide! I think we're too late.' She squinted into the distance, where the sea was beginning to rise around the island.

Nisha felt as if it were coming for her. The sea was closing in, determined not to let her cheat it again. She stood up on the trap and watched its watery arms reaching around the island. The sight of it creeping closer made her throat tighten. Her skin turned cold, but she squeezed the little red stone in her fist.

Down and down into the dark.

'Keep going,' she said. 'Please. We can make it.'

Mrs Barrow hesitated.

'*Please*,' Nisha begged, and this time Mrs Barrow cracked the whip, making Bonny jolt forward with a spurt of speed.

Behind them, Jamie was standing up on the pedals, peering at Barrow Island, and Nisha knew what he was thinking.

'We'll never make it!' he shouted.

'Yes we will!' Nisha shouted back.

Mrs Barrow looked at her and nodded. 'We'll make it. Don't you worry.'

They didn't make it.

47

CAUGHT BY THE TIDE

Before they were even halfway across, it was obvious there was no way they would reach the island before the tide flooded the causeway.

'We'll have to go back,' Mrs Barrow said, slowing down. 'We'll have to turn around.'

Despite her frustration, Nisha knew her grandmother was right. And the sudden reality of being swept away by the tide filled her with a terror that outweighed even the thought of Mr Foster's axe.

The stone causeway was narrow, so Mrs Barrow guided Bonny on to the flats to turn around, but when the wheels thumped down on to the sand, they immediately began to sink. Bonny strained to pull them forward. The muscles bulged in her legs and shoulders, but the wheels hardly moved.

'You can do it, girl.' Mrs Barrow cracked the whip. 'Pull!'

'She'll never do it quick enough.' Jamie jumped off the bike. He ran over to Bonny and grabbed her halter, encouraging the pony to pull harder. 'Tide's comin' too fast.'

The sea was already washing around to touch the landward beach of Barrow Island. And when Nisha turned to look back at the mainland, fear almost swept her away.

'Oh no.' She pointed.

Mrs Barrow stood up in the trap. Jamie climbed up on the side of it and stared.

All three of them knew how much trouble they were in.

The sea had crept around behind them just as Mr Foster said it would. Like a hunter circling its prey. They were now trapped in a patch of beach that was surrounded by the incoming sea. Before long it would close in on them. Nisha could already feel her panic rising. The taste of salt water filled her mouth. The awful memory of suffocation. Of water spilling down her throat. The burning as it filled her lungs.

Down and down into the dark.

'We should have kept going,' Nisha said.

'We should never have come across,' Jamie said. 'I telt you we'd never make it.'

'Only one thing for it.' Mrs Barrow moved to the edge of the trap and climbed down. 'We'll have to get to the refuge hut. Come on. Both of you.'

Nisha didn't need to be told twice. Twig, the Weeping Tree, everything was forgotten now; swept aside by fear. She jumped down, ready to follow her grandmother, but Jamie went straight to Bonny instead.

'What about *her*?' he said. 'We cannot just leave her here.'

'You two are more important,' Mrs Barrow said. 'And you're my responsibility. I'll not let anything happen to you. Not like—'

'I'll not leave her.' Jamie was firm. 'It's not right.' He began to unfasten the buckles on Bonny's harness.

'What are you doing?' Mrs Barrow tried to stop him. 'We don't have time to—'

'I'll not leave her to die!' Jamie pulled away from her.

'All right.' Mrs Barrow looked about, checking the tide. 'Unhitch her from the trap, but hurry up.' She went to help him, working quickly. 'There might just be enough time. And horses can swim, can't they?'

'Aye,' Jamie said as his fingers worked the buckles. 'They're canny swimmers.'

Nisha stayed where she was as the water circled closer.

She wanted to do something, but the thought of the sea washing her away was a concrete weight in her legs. Like before, on the crag, her fear wouldn't let her help. All she could do was watch as Jamie and her grandmother freed Bonny from the harness.

As soon as it was done, Mrs Barrow came back to Nisha and took her hand. 'Don't be afraid,' she said. 'I'll keep you safe. I promise.'

Nisha was starting to hate promises. They only ever led to trouble. And saying 'don't be afraid' didn't stop the fear from bubbling inside her like sea foam around the crag. It didn't stop it from growing until it threatened to fill her completely.

Mrs Barrow dragged Nisha up on to the road and headed towards the refuge hut, but stopped when she realized Jamie wasn't following.

'What are you doing now?' she asked.

Jamie was standing beside Bonny, one hand on the pony's neck. He was watching the sea, scanning all around.

'She'll never swim in this,' Jamie said. 'It's too cold and too far out. The current'll take her.'

'We can't do anything about that.' Mrs Barrow's voice was firm. 'I have to get you to the refuge hut.' She let go of Nisha's hand and stormed back to take Jamie's arm. 'Come along, right now. Don't be so obstinate. I'll not have your death on my conscience as well.'

Nisha felt so exposed, standing there as the sea advanced. So alone and afraid. All she could think of was drowning. Of bombs and fire and people screaming. Of the docks in Singapore. Of Papa being left behind. Of being dragged down and down into the dark.

'Na,' Jamie said. 'I'll not leave her.'

'I'm telling you!' Mrs Barrow tried to pull him away from the pony. 'You're my responsibility. I will *not* let you drown. I will *not* let anything happen to you. Now come with me!'

But Jamie yanked his arm from her grasp. In one quick movement, he snatched a fistful of Bonny's mane, then jumped up and threw his leg over the pony's back. Nisha wouldn't have thought it was possible if she hadn't seen it herself.

'You get to the hut,' Jamie shouted as he kicked his heels and encouraged Bonny up on to the road. 'I'll get Bonny to the island.'

Nisha and Mrs Barrow stood open-mouthed as Jamie kicked his heels once more and galloped away.

The bomb burnt away all the air so I couldn't breathe. Everything was hot, hot, hot. My eyes hurt, my ears hurt, my _whole body_ hurt. And then everything was on fire and the ground disappeared and I was twisting and tumbling. I crashed right into Papa (I think it was Papa) and then I went over the edge of the dock and fell like I was going to fall for ever, and splashed into the sea and went under.

My ears felt like someone had pushed nails into them. Pain went right through my head, but that wasn't the worst thing. The worst thing was that I had no breath in me and that I kept going deeper and deeper. Everything below me was just black. I was sinking down and down into the dark. That's all I could think; down and down into the dark.

The current was sucking me deeper and the light was fading. There were other people in the sea above me all kicking and swimming about in a panic. I got kicked in the ribs. Then I got hit in the head. I couldn't swim up and I knew I was going to drown. I was going to die down there in the dark and it was the most awful thing ever. I was going to open my mouth and breathe in the seawater and it was going to burn its way inside me and kill me. I reached out, grabbing whatever I could. I used other people to drag myself up. I didn't care if I was pulling them down, I kept going until I saw light. And suddenly, for a moment, there was a gap in the bodies above me and I swam towards it and then I was bursting out of the waves and breathing the hot, stinking air.

I was alive, coughing and spluttering, but there were people all around me in the water – swimming, sinking, or just floating there all bloody and horrible, being washed about by the waves. There was only a narrow gap of sea between the dock and the hull of the ship. If the waves pushed the ship up against the dock, there would be nowhere for us to go. It was going to crush us or force us underwater to drown. Everyone was desperate to get away. Some were trying to swim away to escape the ship. Others were trying to climb the dock wall, but it was too slimy and they were slipping back down on top of the others. People were climbing over each other, pushing each other down, not caring.

And there was David Hill. He was right in the middle of everyone, with his head above the waves. His eyes were staring in panic. There was no sign of his amma. David was treading water, but people kept bumping into him and he kept going under and coming back up again with his mouth opening and closing as if he was shouting. That's when I realized I couldn't hear anything. I can now. Out of one ear. But then, I couldn't hear anything at all except for a kind of rushing sound. Then someone pushed past me, pressing down on my shoulder so I went under again. My mouth filled up with seawater that burnt in my throat, and panic flooded through me.

I kicked and kicked and pushed myself up towards the frothing surface, desperate to escape. And when I came back up I was facing the dock and I saw Papa standing up there with the crowd. There was blood all over his face and shirt, and black smoke and fire behind him. He was looking right at me and I wanted to be with him more than anything in the whole world. I knew he would save me because that's what papas do and mine is the best of all. He shouted something then threw a rope to me. Amma was there too, ready to help, but it was a long way up to the dock, with no way to climb other than that rope. When the people around me saw it they all swam towards it, pushing and shoving and kicking each other to get the rope first.

I didn't stand a chance.

48
REFUGE

Already the water was over Nisha's boots. Further along the path, spray was exploding from beneath Bonny's hooves as she galloped along the causeway.

'That boy's going to get himself killed,' Mrs Barrow said.

The wind was picking up, blustering over the island and down across the sands. Mrs Barrow's hat brim fluttered and she had to hold on to it to stop it from flying away. The hem of her coat lifted and flapped around her legs. Nisha's hair whipped about her face.

'Quickly.' Mrs Barrow grasped Nisha's hand once more and the two of them hurried towards the refuge hut.

Salt water splashed around them with every step. It soaked Nisha's boots and flicked up the backs of her legs. Soon it was over her ankles and numbing her feet.

'Hurry!' Mrs Barrow was frantic.

The sea rushed in without mercy.

'Almost there!'

The freezing, grey water washed around Nisha's knees. It sucked at her, trying to pull her over. Her coat-tails floated like drowned spirits. The sand beneath her feet softened and drew her down. It was becoming harder to move. Soon their only option would be to swim, and by then it would be too late.

The sea was at Nisha's waist by the time they made it to the rickety steps.

She let go of her grandmother's hand and scrambled up, clinging to the handrail. The wood was slippery with seaweed. Tiny shells clung to the slimy steps, crunching under her boots. When she reached the top, Nisha wished there was higher to climb. She wished she could clamber further and further away from the sea. She was so certain it was going to keep coming after her. That it would chase her for ever and ever until it had finally dragged her into its cold, dark depths.

Down and down into the dark.

Cold and wet, Nisha tumbled into the hut and fell to the floor. She wrapped both arms around herself. Her mind spun as if she were set adrift on a boat. She felt the hut break free from its stilts and pirouette with the incoming current. They were cast adrift and would be washed away.

She closed her eyes and told herself it wasn't happening.

'Well, that was an adventure,' Mrs Barrow said, coming to stand beside her and look out of the window. 'But we're safe now.'

Nisha dared to open her eyes.

They were not afloat on the sea. They were above the waves, safe for now in a hut that was smaller than the tree house. It was nothing more than a narrow shed bolted on to four thick wooden stilts that rooted it to the seabed. Three sides were fitted with windows, the glass long since cracked. The fourth side was an open doorway. There was almost no protection from the howling wind.

'It's quite beautiful really,' Mrs Barrow said. 'If you think about it.'

Nisha saw that her grandmother was pretending she wasn't scared. Putting on a brave face. Joy said everyone did it these days. Nisha remembered what Papa told her the day they fled from the plantation and left their life behind. He had said that being brave wasn't not being scared. It was being scared but finding a way to carry on.

Courage is conquering fear.

And Nisha saw that was what her grandmother was

doing. She was finding a way to conquer her fear – for Nisha's sake.

So Nisha made herself stand up beside her grandmother. She forced her legs to move and she used the wooden windowsill to pull herself to her feet. Then she reached out and took her grandmother's hand.

'We'll be fine now,' Mrs Barrow said.

'Yes,' Nisha managed.

Beyond the window, the causeway was gone and Papa's bicycle was lost beneath the waves. The trap was listing to one side and turning as the sea carried it away. Closer to the island, Jamie was nearing the dunes. He looked smudged and smeary through the dirty, cracked windows. Bonny was no longer galloping – the water was too deep for that. Mostly, she was underwater, the waves buffeting around her flanks. Nisha couldn't even see the pony's legs. But Jamie pushed her on until she reached the beach and came up out of the water.

'He made it,' Mrs Barrow said. 'He actually made it.'

Nisha felt the lightness of relief when Jamie rode Bonny clear of the surf. Then he turned and raised one arm, waving it from side to side.

'He's quite the horseman,' Mrs Barrow said.

'Yes, he is.' Nisha felt proud to be his friend.

Jamie turned and galloped away along the beach and on to the path towards Barrow House. Nisha watched him until he faded into the greying evening. When he was gone, she scanned the silhouette of the island, seeing a figure standing near the north end.

Nisha stared at him just standing there, and wondered what it meant. She was sure that if Mr Foster had cut down the Weeping Tree, Twig would have been cut down with it. He was, after all, the heart of the tree.

So perhaps something had stopped Mr Foster's axe.

With a glimmer of hope in her heart, Nisha glanced across to see that her grandmother was staring at the same spot, where the north end of the island rose from the sea. She was frowning as if she wasn't sure what she was looking at.

'What do you see?' Nisha asked.

'I'm . . .' Mrs Barrow shook her head. 'I'm not sure. I thought . . . No, it can't be.' A single tear slipped from the corner of her eye. She wiped it away with a gloved hand. 'No. It can't be.'

49
SECRETS

Wind howled around the hut. It blew in through the open doorway, whistling between the gaps in the planks. Cracked glass rattled in the windows.

The sky darkened as evening brought mist rolling in over the sea, and then it was as if they were the only two people alive in the world.

They wrung the seawater out of their dresses and coats as best they could, then Nisha walked once around the hut, inspecting their tiny place of refuge. She tried not to look out at the water surrounding them. Every time she did, it made her stomach churn and her head spin.

There was a first aid box bolted to one wall. A black

tin with a drop-down front. There wasn't much inside: a couple of open-wove bandages, a red tin of aromatic ammonia and some zinc ointment. There were also two candles and a box of matches. Beside the first aid kit was an orange life ring with a length of greasy rope attached to it.

Hanging from a nail in one corner of the hut was a lamp that creaked as it swung from side to side.

Nisha sat down on the hard floor and rested her back against the wall. She was sheltered from the wind, but still felt the thump of every wave that crashed around the wooden stilts just inches below her. She put a numb hand into her damp pocket and fumbled for the red stone. Pulling it out, she held it tight in her fist as she tried not to imagine a powerful surge of seawater pushing the hut over and spilling her into its cold grasp.

Down and down into the dark.

'What have you got there?' Mrs Barrow eased herself to the floor opposite Nisha. She shivered and adjusted her coat, trying to give herself something soft to sit on.

Nisha hadn't shared the stone with anybody but Twig. No one other than he knew it was there.

'It's fine if you want to keep it to yourself,' Mrs Barrow said, rubbing her hands together for warmth. 'We all have our secrets.'

Nisha looked up at her. 'It's a stone.'

Mrs Barrow nodded.

'From home,' Nisha said. 'It's the only thing I have left.'

'I'm so sorry for what's happened to you.' Mrs Barrow sighed.

Nisha looked down at the stone in her hand.

'You've come such a long way,' said her grandmother. 'And I haven't exactly been very welcoming, have I? It's been strange for me to have new people in the house. Especially you, because . . .' Mrs Barrow put her hand to her mouth and tapped her lips with her fingers. 'Because . . .' She turned her head and closed her eyes.

Nisha knew what people looked like when they were trying not to cry, so she said nothing.

She waited.

Eventually her grandmother opened her eyes again and looked directly at Nisha. She took a deep breath and said, 'It's been especially difficult because you remind me so much of Elizabeth.'

50

MRS BARROW'S TRUTH

'Elizabeth was full of life,' Mrs Barrow said. 'Always wanting to be outside, running about in the fresh air.' The trace of a smile touched her lips then faded. 'And she did love that wretched tree house.'

Elizabeth Barrow.

The name on the seat in the flower garden. And on the headstone in the churchyard.

Mrs Barrow crossed her arms over her chest and trembled in the cold. 'I've been thinking about Elizabeth ever such a lot since you arrived,' she said. 'That must be why I lost track of time at the churchyard. I was trying to remember all the little things I had forgotten about her.

Like the way she pulled at the collar of her dress.'

'Who was she?' Nisha asked. But even as she said it, Nisha realized she already knew. The plaque in the garden, the secret room, the headstone. But, most of all, the photograph in grandmother's study. Nisha had been too wrapped up in worrying about Amma, and in trying to find Twig's treasures, to realize what she had seen and what those things meant.

'She was Papa's sister,' Nisha said.

'Your father never told you?'

Nisha shook her head and tightened her fist around the red stone.

'It was a very hard time for him. He didn't talk about it. Not ever. He could never come to terms with what happened. I think that's what drove him away from here in the end.' Mrs Barrow stood up. She rubbed the window with the cuff of her coat and looked out. Dark wings were spreading over Barrow Island. Another hour or so and it would be lost to the night.

As Nisha watched her grandmother, she realized something important. She had always thought that as she grew older, there would be less to worry about. She would be able to do as she pleased, and never have to feel bad about anything. But now she saw that children weren't the only ones to have worries. They weren't the only ones to have fear and guilt and pain and sadness. Even people as old as her grandmother had those things inside them.

'Elizabeth was my daughter,' Mrs Barrow said. 'Your father's twin sister. She would have been your aunt. She was such an energetic, solitary thing, always wanting to be outside. I used to say she was like a cat, but she always said she was more like a boy. I think she wanted more than anything to be a boy.' Mrs Barrow stopped, as if she didn't want to go on.

Nisha waited, teeth chattering in the cold.

The wind howled. The sea crashed.

After a time, Mrs Barrow cleared her throat. 'She wanted us to call her "Eli" instead of Elizabeth, but it sounded so . . . *awful*. Elizabeth is such a beautiful name. And there was no use trying to make her wear a dress, because she would scratch and tug at the collar, or she would simply steal clothes from her brother's wardrobe. So we agreed that she would wear a dress when she was off the island, and do as she pleased when she was here.'

'I saw a photograph on your desk,' Nisha said. 'That's her, isn't it?'

'Ah yes, you were in my study.' Mrs Barrow turned around. 'Exploring, I suppose?' A faint smile crept to the corner of her mouth. 'Elizabeth would've done the same. You know, I dug out that old photograph just after you arrived. To remind myself. I made her wear a dress that day and she hated me for it.'

'And that's Elizabeth's room at the top of the house,' Nisha said.

'You've been in there too, haven't you?' Mrs Barrow didn't look surprised. 'That was you I saw that day?'

'Yes.' Nisha lowered her eyes. She felt the painful stab of guilt that she had stolen the key. But at least she had owned up to it. The guilt about David Hill cut much deeper. She had never been able to own up to *that*.

'I've kept her room the way she liked it,' said Mrs Barrow. 'And I put fresh flowers there whenever I can.' She paused for a moment before taking a deep breath. 'The only thing we ever had in common was the flower garden. She loved flowers, but daphnes were always her favourite.'

Mrs Barrow pulled a handkerchief from her sleeve. Untouched by the sea, it was still dry, so she used it to dab her eyes. 'I blame myself. I should have been stricter with her. I should have watched her more carefully. I should have banned her from the north end of the island and kept her in the house.'

Nisha looked up at her grandmother. 'What happened?'

'The Weeping Tree wasn't always so close to the crag. When my grandfather built the tree house, the tree was much further back from the edge. The Keep, too. Except it's not a real keep, you know? It's a "folly". My grandfather built it to catch the eye. The Victorians liked to do silly things like that. But the rock was weak and decades of wind and sea wore it down. When the cliff collapsed, Elizabeth fell with it. The sea took her away from me,

Nisha. It took her away and all I have now is an empty grave in the churchyard and a bench in the garden. And her room, of course. I should have forbidden her from the tree house. I should have done something, but instead she . . .' Mrs Barrow stopped to compose herself.

'It was my fault,' she said after a while. 'I should have cut down that tree long before anything could happen, but after she was gone, I left it there because she loved it. And to remind myself that I was to blame. When I saw that boy fall, though, I knew I couldn't let it happen again. That's why I told Mr Foster to cut it down.'

'But you can't. Not now.'

'No. What you said is right. If I lose the tree, I lose a part of Elizabeth. She loved it, and now it stands as a memorial to her. One that's better than any bench or headstone or empty room. I understand that now.'

Nisha felt an ache in her heart for her grandmother. What a terrible thing to weigh her down. She wondered if Elizabeth had known Twig. Had Twig tried to save Elizabeth the way he had tried to save Jamie? But Twig had only been able to do so much. Mr Foster had done the rest. Nisha imagined Elizabeth alone on the crag, falling to her death with no one to see her. No one to help.

Mrs Barrow dabbed her eyes again and looked down at Nisha.

Outside, rain began to fall. It spit-spattered on the

windows, growing harder and faster with every second that passed.

'You're wearing one of her dresses,' Mrs Barrow said. 'It was the only thing we had that would fit you. And every time you pull at the neck, I can see Elizabeth. She used to do exactly the same thing. She said it itched and she hated it. And she had the same look in her eyes, the same way of biting her lip, the same frown. Every time I look at you, I see Elizabeth. And I blame myself for what happened.'

Nisha stood up and put her arms around her grandmother.

Sometimes, when words are not enough, a hug is the only way to tell someone you care.

Extract from Nisha Barrow's Truth, 1942

Amma screamed at the man who grabbed the rope meant for me. I'll never forget his bald white head bobbing up and down in the waves while everyone splashed and tried to get to the rope. But the bald man got there first and refused to let go. I thought he was bad and mean but then he reached out and held on to me. He shouted up to Amma and Papa, who pulled as hard as they could, dragging us both through the water. As soon as we came to the side of the dock, the man helped me wrap my arms around his neck then held on to the rope with both hands and put his feet against the side of the wall. Like that, he half walked half climbed up the slimy dock with me clinging to his back, while Amma and Papa pulled.

As soon as we reached the top, the bald man let go of me then threw the rope back into the water to help the others. I'd thought at first that he was a bad man but I was wrong. He was a good, brave man and I wonder where he is now. I wonder if he survived the docks. I wonder if he has children.

Papa picked me up straight away. Amma was touching me and wiping my hair from my face and checking me. I stared down into the water at all the people still trying to escape. It was the most horrible thing. All those people so scared. But there was no sign of David Hill any more. He was gone. Just gone. The sea had taken him. Down and down into the dark. I knew he was under the waves, underneath all those desperate people, filled with seawater and sinking. He would never make another joke or say another word or take another breath. He didn't deserve that. No one deserves that. I felt awful and so _guilty_ for letting him take the blame for what I'd done, throwing that rock. His papa hit him for it and now he was dead, and David was dead, and there was no sign of his amma. I'd never be able to say sorry. It's still there, scratching away at me, and there's nothing I'll ever be able to do about it so I'm saying it now. I'm sorry, David Hill. I'm sorry, I'm sorry, I'm sorry.

Amma and Papa took me away from it all. They carried me through the crowd, saying something but I couldn't hear what it was. I put a hand to my right ear and a horrible pain shot through my head, and when I looked at my fingers, there was blood on them. It hurt for ages after that and I still can't hear from my right ear but at least I'm alive.

Amma and Papa took me through the crowd towards the man in uniform with the list. Some of his soldiers were shoving people back, keeping them away from the steps, while others were preparing to withdraw the gangplank.

Papa put me down but everything was woozy by then. I could hardly even walk. There was blood coming out of my ear and my whole body was hurting. Papa crouched and held my face in his hands and said something to me. I couldn't hear what it was but I could see his lips moving and I know he was telling me to be brave, to have courage, to look after Amma. I didn't understand why he was saying that. Then he stood up and pushed me and Amma on to the gangplank.

Amma dragged me on board the ship. Almost as soon as she stepped foot on the deck, the whole thing lurched and when I looked back, I realized the Empress of India was already sliding away from the dock and out to sea. Standing in the crowd below, still on land, Papa was looking up at me.

'No!' I shouted. 'No!' But it was already too late and all I could do was stand against the railings on deck and watch as we left him behind. I kept my eyes on Papa until he was no more than a tiny dot. Even then, I kept watch as Singapore disappeared and the Empress of India headed away at full steam.

51

THE GOLDEN MOON

A low, sad clanging sound drifted through the rain. 'Do you hear that?' Mrs Barrow looked up. She and Nisha were sitting side by side, wet and miserable, pressed into one corner of the hut to protect themselves from the biting wind.

'I don't hear ... Wait.' Nisha turned her head. 'Is that a bell?'

'A bell,' her grandmother confirmed.

They stood and looked out towards the island, squinting into the fret.

It wasn't night yet, but evening was advancing on them like an army of darkness. Everything was grey, and

Barrow Island was invisible.

'Do you see anything?' Mrs Barrow asked.

Nisha shook her head. She saw only rain and fret, and the sea in turmoil inches below the hut.

'Mr Foster wouldn't dare come out in this mist, would he?' said Mrs Barrow.

'We should light the lamp.' With her hands shaking from the cold, Nisha opened the first aid tin and took out a candle and the box of matches. 'So he knows where we are.'

She lifted the lamp from its hook, jammed the candle into the holder, then put it on the floor in the corner to protect it from the wind as she lit it. Her numb fingers were awkward but the match flared on her third strike and the smell of burning phosphorus brought back a sudden and clear memory of lighting incense in Malaya, to keep the mosquitoes away at night.

Fat lot of good that had done. It hadn't kept them away from Amma.

Nisha closed the lamp's little door, then hung it on the hook so it swung backwards and forwards in the window.

Seeing the yellowy-orange glow, Nisha had a sudden thought. 'What if bombers come? What if they see the light?'

'They'd be lucky to see anything in this weather,' Mrs Barrow said. 'I'm not sure even Mr Foster will see it.'

As if to prove her wrong, a call came through the rain. 'Ahoy!' It sounded hollow in the eerie evening.

Nisha and Mrs Barrow looked out, seeing mist swirl around the choppy surface of the waves.

The bell rang again, low and melancholy, then . . .

'I think I see a light.' Nisha breathed on the cracked window and rubbed it with her sleeve. 'Do you see?'

'I see it. Quickly! Bring the lamp closer.'

Nisha grabbed the lamp and put it closer to the window. She waved it from side to side.

'Ahoy!' the voice came again, and this time Mrs Barrow replied. 'Ahoy!'

She took the lamp from Nisha and went to the doorway. 'Ahoy!' She swung it so the lamp flickered in the mist.

Nisha stayed back, afraid to go too close. The sea was just a few steps below, swirling and churning and frothing. One wrong step, one slippery board, and she could go in. And she knew that once the sea had her, it would never let her go.

Not this time.

'We're here!' Mrs Barrow called into the evening, and then Nisha saw the bow of a small boat appear from the mist. A lamp swung from a pole fixed to the bow, and a sombre bell rang each time a fierce wave rocked the hull.

And there was Mr Foster, looking over his shoulder as he rowed towards them.

Nisha's heart thumped harder with each lift and dip of the oars. She knew what was going to happen. She would have to climb into the boat as it rose and fell in the water.

'You'll have to be quick!' Mr Foster shouted. As he came close, he let go of the oars and used a rope to moor the boat to the handrail of the refuge hut. 'It's gettin' worse.'

'We're safe now,' Mrs Barrow said to Nisha, but her face darkened when she saw the fear in her granddaughter's eyes. 'What is it? What's wrong?'

Nisha shook her head and backed away. 'I can't. I'm afraid.'

'Hurry up!' Mr Foster stumbled as the boat swept sideways.

Mrs Barrow put the lamp on the floor and edged out on to the first step. The sea was inches from her shoes. She turned and held her hand towards Nisha.

'I won't let anything happen to you,' she said. 'You'll be safe with me.'

Nisha was too afraid to leave, and too afraid to stay.

The wind was building, and the waves were growing. The water crashed around the wooden stilts of the refuge hut. The spray spattered against the windows. It filled the air. It was everywhere, and Nisha knew the sea didn't want her to leave. It wanted to steal her down into its depths the way it had stolen Elizabeth Barrow.

She looked from her grandmother to the small rowing boat moored to the steps. Rising and falling. Rising and falling.

Thump. Thump. Thump.

The hull nudged against the wood like the devil knocking at Nisha's door.

Mr Foster stood at the bow of the boat, one hand on the gunwale to keep him steady, the other beckoning to them.

'Hurry up!' he shouted. 'The sea's gettin' worse.'

The swell was much bigger than before. It rose and fell like mountains. Every third or fourth wave washed over the top step as if it would keep rising until it drowned the refuge hut.

'It's all right,' Mrs Barrow shouted. 'You get in first. I'll help you—'

And then she was gone.

The sea reached up to take her before she could finish her sentence. Watery hands wrapped around her ankles and pulled her legs from under her. Her hat whipped away in the wind, and Nisha could only watch in horror as her grandmother slipped out to sea.

Nisha froze. Her inner self put down roots and fixed her to the floor. She couldn't bear to acknowledge what had happened to her grandmother, so her mind began to close down, blocking all the terrible images.

And in that overwhelming darkness, Nisha thought about Papa. She remembered what he had said about courage: that it was about conquering fear.

If there was ever a time to be brave, it was now.

Nisha forced herself to move. She tore her roots from the wooden boards beneath her feet and shuffled forwards, clinging to the door frame as she emerged on to the top step.

Mr Foster was standing up in the rowing boat. Rain-soaked and desperate, he looked first over one side, then over the other.

'Do you see her?' he called to Nisha. 'Where is she?' His clothes were drenched. His hat was gone. The little rowing boat rose and fell, sweeping from side to side, knocking on the steps.

Thump. Thump. Thump.

'Where is she?' He looked at Nisha only for a moment before he went back to searching.

Nisha forced herself to look beyond the rowing boat at the turmoil of the sea. And there, in the nightmare of mist and rain, was her grandmother.

She was trying to swim, but the waves smashed in her face, filling her mouth. Nisha could almost feel the tired-ness in her grandmother's muscles. She was fading quickly.

'There.' She pointed. 'I see her!'

Mr Foster looked back at Nisha then followed the line of her finger. 'Where? I can't see a thing through this mist.'

But Nisha saw no mist. As on the night she had made the agreement with Twig, the world slowed as if in a dream. The mist faded, the rain hung in the air, the sea calmed, and the sky cleared. The waves were suddenly bright and glittering in the moonlight. And then she realized.

The moon.

It was full and bright and round.

And golden.

Time was running out, hope was fading, and there were still treasures to find. But Twig was showing her the way. He wanted her to help Mrs Barrow. Perhaps *she* was the treasure.

'Right there!' Nisha pointed again. Her grandmother was drifting further and further from the boat and the refuge hut. The waves were drawing her away as if they wanted to drag her to the deepest North Sea.

Down and down into the dark.

'I can't see a bloody thing!' Mr Foster yelled. 'Not a thing!'

Nisha knew that if she didn't act now, the sea would take her grandmother.

Like it had taken David Hill.

Like it had taken Elizabeth.

52
DOWN AND DOWN INTO THE DARK

Slipping and sliding on the wet boards, Nisha hurried back into the hut. She plucked the life ring from the hook beside the first aid box, bundled the coiled rope into her arms, and made her way back to the open doorway.

Outside, the sea raged and the wind blustered. But still the golden moon flickered on the waves like fire.

Nisha secured the loose end of the rope to the handrail of the steps. She pulled it once to make sure it was tight.

'I don't see her!' Mr Foster was holding on to the gunwale as the rowing boat lurched from side to side. He was leaning so far over, one good surge would topple him in.

'I do,' Nisha yelled back.

She was terrified. Her inner roots threatened to spread out and fix her to the spot, but there was no time to waste. The rising and falling waves were a ticking clock. Each time the water swelled, more precious seconds slipped away.

There was only one way to save her grandmother.

Nisha took off her coat and threw it into the rowing boat. She then slipped the life ring over her head.

'What are you doing?' Mr Foster's expression was shock and disbelief. 'You can't—'

Nisha didn't hear what he said next. She heard only the wind, then the muted rush of bubbles as she hit the surface of the water and went under.

It was another world beneath the waves. A world of cold, black movement.

Her heart jolted to a sudden stop. The shock of the freezing water made her chest tighten as if the North Sea would crush her heart into the tiniest grain of sand. And then it would swallow her.

Down and down into the dark.

But the beat came back with a strength Nisha had never known. It hammered like a fist on her ribcage. And as it did, the life ring drew Nisha back up to the surface so that she burst out into the open and took a deep breath of sea air.

She rose and fell on the waves, turning in a circle,

searching for her grandmother.

Frothy fingers grasped at her mouth and nose. Tongues of seaweed wrapped around her legs. The sea embraced her and tried to pull her down, but Nisha kicked hard, turning and searching.

There!

Not far away, her grandmother was treading water. The waves were washing over her, throwing her sideways.

Nisha struck out towards her. She put all her strength into cutting through the water. She could hardly believe she was here, but all thoughts of drowning were gone now. She had only one thing to do.

She pushed on through the water, fighting the current, edging closer and closer to her grandmother.

But Mrs Barrow was weakening. Her muscles were slowing.

Nisha saw her grandmother vanish below the surface. She came up for breath but her movements were feeble and when she slipped out of sight again, she didn't reappear.

Down and down into the dark.

'No!'

Nisha put every ounce of strength into those last few strokes. Everything she had.

She reached the spot where her grandmother had disappeared, and she let herself slip down through the ring. She reached up with one hand to keep hold of the rope, and searched the depths with her other hand. Grasping. Grabbing. Hoping against hope.

Please, Twig, she thought. *Please.*

And then her fist closed around something floating in the current.

Nisha tightened her grip and pulled.

Up and up into the moonlight, Mrs Barrow surfaced like driftwood. But she was still alive. She was still breathing. A moment longer and she would have been gone for ever.

Nisha wrapped one arm around her, and hooked the other into the life ring.

'Pull!' she screamed. 'Pull us in!'

She felt a tug and looked back to see Mr Foster hauling the rope towards him. He dragged them through the water until they were beside the boat, then he reached down to take hold of Mrs Barrow.

Her grandmother had very little strength left in her, so Nisha clung to the handrail of the refuge hut and put her feet on the submerged steps to help. The waves battered her, trying their utmost to wash her from her perch, but she held firm.

'We have to get her back to the house!' Mr Foster shouted. 'She'll catch her death out here!'

In the golden light, Nisha and Mr Foster helped Mrs Barrow climb aboard, then Nisha hauled herself into the boat and cast off the rope that held it secure.

'Is the tree still standing?' she asked.

Mr Foster was confused by the question.

'The Weeping Tree,' Nisha shouted. 'Did you cut it down?'

'No,' he said. 'That thing is like steel. Blunted me axe with just a few strokes. And the wind – it nearly blew us over the crag. It's like it didn't want us to cut it down.'

53

THE SILVER MOON

Mrs Barrow sat hunched and wretched at the stern of the boat while Mr Foster put all his strength into rowing her home.

From the bow, Nisha watched the golden moon that hung over the island. But with every creak of the oars and every slap of the sea against the hull, the gold faded. The moon was turning, becoming silver. Nisha knew that soon her time would be up.

She had found only one of the three treasures. Hope was almost gone.

But as her heart grew heavier with the prospect of failure, she felt a warmth around her wrist. And when she pushed up the sleeve of her dress to look at the bracelet, hope reignited.

Two words now glowed in the grain.

With a burst of excitement, she twisted the bracelet to read the second word. Written in the same scrolling script, and glowing with the same fire, it was unmistakeable.

virtus.

Nisha put her hand over the bracelet and closed her eyes. She had somehow found the second treasure. There was just one more to find.

But the moon. The gold.

Her eyes snapped open and she saw the moon hanging in the sky. Now it was hardly gold at all. Soon it would be just silver and ordinary. Like a shiny shilling.

'We have to go faster!' she called to Mr Foster. 'Please!'

'I'm gannin' as fast as I can,' he shouted back. 'I'm not gettin' any younger.'

Nisha scrambled past him to get to her grandmother.

'What does "virtus" mean?' she asked.

'Hmm?' Mrs Barrow looked up. Her wet hair hung across her brow. Her eyes were bloodshot, and she was shivering wildly.

'"Virtus". What does it mean? What language is it?'

'It's L-Latin,' Mrs Barrow stuttered through chattering teeth. 'B-but why—'

'What does it *mean?*'

Confused, Mrs Barrow managed to say, 'C-courage. It m-means courage.'

Nisha let the word sink in as she turned to watch the sky. She had found honesty, and she had found courage. Only one more treasure eluded her, but she was already too late.

Hanging high over Barrow Island, the moon was silver. Not a trace of gold was left in it.

As they neared the beach, Nisha saw Twig one more time.

He was just a dark shape standing at the north end of the island, beneath the silver moon. Tears filled Nisha's eyes as she watched him.

Twig was her only hope of making Amma better. Her only hope to save Papa.

But she had failed.

As they reached Barrow Island, and the hull of the boat ground into the sand, Nisha looked down at the two words etched into the bracelet. The letters no longer glowed like fire. They were losing their lustre, turning cold like everything else Nisha had encountered since arriving on Barrow Island.

'No,' she sobbed. 'Please.'

But the clouds were gathering across the moon and Twig was fading. His shape was merging with the rain. He raised a hand, then turned and walked away, disappearing into the darkness.

'No.'

Behind her, Mr Foster was helping Mrs Barrow to her feet. 'We'll get you straight up to the house,' he was saying. 'You too, young lassie. Mrs F will draw you a warm bath and fetch you a hot drink. The pair of you must be freezin' cold. Soon as the tide's back out again, we'll send for Doc Michaels to check you over.'

Dazed and unthinking, Nisha waded on to the beach. She stood looking up towards the north end of the island.

'Oh, that's just what we need,' said Mr Foster as he brought Mrs Barrow ashore. 'You hear that? Why won't that bloody Hitler just leave us alone?'

Nisha hardly heard the bombers, but she felt them in the air. The night vibrated with the hum of their engines.

'Come on,' Mr Foster said. 'We'd better be quick before they start droppin' bombs on us.'

'No,' Nisha said. 'There's something I have to do.'

And without looking back, she ran.

Her dress was heavy with seawater. The hem rubbed against her legs, and the neckline chafed her skin. Her boots squelched with every step, and the rain punished her, but Nisha didn't slow and she didn't stop. She sprinted up the beach and on to the road towards the house.

She could hear the bombers now. They had passed the island and ripped through the stormy night towards the headland. Already the searchlights were glowing in the clouds. Already the anti-aircraft guns were playing their music.

Nisha's pounding boots joined the night orchestra, battling the thump of her heart. She breathed hard, sucking down the cold air and huffing it out in time with her steps. She followed the road until she met the path that led to the walled garden.

Tears washed from her eyes to join the rain. They blurred her vision but she still didn't pause. She ran along the path and barged into the walled garden. She splashed between the rows of vegetables and stumbled into the flower garden.

There, the smell was unreal. The overwhelming scent of daphnes filled her. Rich and sweet. It felt warm in her chest and gave her new energy. Twig *had* to listen to her. He *had* to give her one more chance.

With that fresh burst of encouragement, Nisha swept through the curtain of ivy that concealed the way on to the overgrown path through the gorse.

Further down the coast, the bombers were doing their terrible work. Fires flickered in the sky. The world trembled.

Nisha bolted towards the crag, her breath coming in tight gasps, and when she reached the end of the path, she fell to her knees in front of the Weeping Tree.

'Please,' she shouted into the rain. 'Please. Just one more chance.'

But no one was there.

There was only the distant hum and flash of flame.

'Please.' Nisha scanned the tree, searching for a sign. A change in temperature, a shift of shadow, a rustle of leaves.

But there was nothing.

Twig was gone.

54
ONE MORE PROMISE

Still on her knees, Nisha hung her head and let her rain-drenched hair cover her face. She closed her eyes and felt her tears wash away.

'Please,' she whispered. 'Just one more chance.'

'You're too late.' The voice was like the breeze.

Nisha opened her eyes and looked up at Twig.

'And you broke your promise.'

'No,' Nisha said. 'No. I—'

'You spoke my name three times. The last time, in the churchyard, was the loudest.'

'I-I tried not to but – it just came out,' Nisha said. 'Everything was going wrong. They were going to cut down the tree and I had to do something. They were going to cut it down because of what happened to Jamie and Elizabeth.'

'Elizabeth?' Twig frowned and looked away.

'Elizabeth Barrow.' Nisha hardly noticed the sound of the planes growing louder. She was concentrating too hard on Twig. She believed that if she looked away from him, even for a fraction of a second, he would disappear once more.

'Elizabeth Barrow?' Twig repeated the name. His frown softened and his eyes widened in sudden understanding. 'Elizabeth Barrow.'

Twig turned to Nisha and his eyes twinkled silver. He put his cold hands on either side of her face. When he spoke, there was something different in his voice. Something less distant.

'You're too late,' he said. 'But you came anyway.'

'Yes.'

The sound of the planes was overwhelming now. It vibrated in Nisha's chest, but she heard only Twig's voice. She saw only his eyes.

'You broke your promise,' he said. 'But you came anyway.'

'Yes.'

'You had hope,' he said.

And when he said it, Nisha felt a warmth on her wrist. With a surge of excitement, she pulled back the sleeve of her dress and saw the letters glowing on the bracelet. But there were three words now.

Three.

'You brought them,' Twig said. 'You found all three.'

'I don't understand.'

'You had hope,' he said. 'When it seemed as if all was lost. You found hope.'

She focused on the word that had appeared on the bracelet.

spes.

And as she stared, the bracelet began to crumble. The words faded to nothing and the wood turned to ash that blew away on the wind.

'Everything will be all right now,' Twig told her. 'I promise.'

The planes were overhead. Right over the island. Nisha didn't hear them, though. She didn't see them. She didn't hear the whistle of the stray bomb because she couldn't look away from Twig as he leant into the moonlight and she saw his features clearly for the first time. Because, all of a sudden, everything made sense. Nisha had seen his face before, in daylight, staring out from a photograph. And he was so much more than just the heart of the Weeping Tree.

'Thank you,' Twig said. 'For helping me remember who I am.'

Nisha nodded.

'Will you do one more thing for me? There's something I need you to say to someone.'

'Yes,' Nisha said. 'Anything. I promise.'

As Twig finished telling Nisha what he wanted her to say, there was a blinding flash of light. In an instant, everything was fire and noise and chaos. Nisha felt herself lift from the ground and spin head over heels, twisting like a rag doll. Pain flared in her head. Fire burnt in her joints. Her eyes bulged and her insides ached. The air sucked away from her lungs. Dirt and grit and rock filled her world.

55

AMMA

Nisha stumbled along the path and into the seclu-
sion of the flower garden. Her whole body burnt
with pain. Her movements were slow and confused.

She had been lying in the grass when she woke. The
force of Hitler's bomb had lifted her off her feet and
thrown her into the gorse. She was bleeding from her
head, and her face was numb, but she was alive.

The rain had slowed to a drizzle, and there was just
enough moonlight to see that the Keep was gone. It no
longer stood on the northernmost tip of the island
because the northernmost tip had collapsed into the sea.
But the Weeping Tree remained. Like a twisted hand it

still reached up into the sky. And the tree house rested like a toy in its palm.

Nisha made her way through the garden, and when she stepped out on to the path that led to Barrow House, she saw four figures coming towards her out of the darkness.

They stopped only when they were almost on top of her.

'Good Lord!' Her grandmother hugged her so hard Nisha's face pressed right against her bosom. 'We were searching for you in the house and then we heard . . .' She stopped and released Nisha, holding her at arm's length as if to inspect her. 'You're bleeding . . .'

'Did ya hear the bomb?' Jamie was saying. 'I mean, of course ya heard the bomb, but did ya see it? Where did it hit? The whole island shook like . . .'

'We need to get her inside,' Mrs F was fussing. 'You too, Mrs Barrow. You shouldn't even be out here. I need to get you both into a good hot bath and . . .'

'. . . Keep's gone from the look of it . . .' Mr Foster's voice was there too. '. . . lucky to be alive . . .'

But Nisha pulled herself from her grandmother's hands and continued in her daze towards Barrow House.

The others followed, fussing over her, but Nisha ignored their questions. She concentrated on putting one foot in front of the other until she came to the house and pushed in through the front door.

Her boots clomped on the stones in the entrance hall, and she left a line of muddy footprints as she headed for the main staircase. A few days ago, Nisha would have worried about the mess, but not today. There was only one thing she cared about right now.

'Nisha?'

She stopped with her foot on the first step and looked up.

The figure standing at the top of the staircase was dressed in a long white nightgown. Her black hair hung lank and lifeless around her pale, drawn face. Her eyes were sunken, her lips were thin, and the fingers that gripped the bannister were narrow and bony.

For one awful moment, Nisha thought she was looking at a ghost.

'Nisha?' she said again. 'What was that noise? I heard a terrible noise and woke up and—'

Nisha didn't hear the rest. She raced up to throw her arms around Amma. She squeezed her tight and faded into her mother's warmth.

Amma put her face on the top of Nisha's head and hugged her in return.

'You're wet,' she said. 'And bleeding. What happened to you?'

'It doesn't matter,' Nisha said.

And it really didn't matter.

56

ELIZABETH BARROW

By eleven o'clock the tide was out, so Jamie took Bonny and rode through the moonlight to fetch Doctor Michaels.

On their return, Jamie waited in the kitchen with Mr Foster. He had a cup of tea, a slice of cake and no complaints whatsoever.

Doctor Michaels came upstairs to examine Amma, and when he was finished, he stood beside the bed scratching his head as if it didn't quite make sense. 'The fever's broken,' he said. 'It's the strangest thing.'

Amma looked up from where she lay and smiled weakly. 'Thank you, Doctor.'

'I admit it's not what I expected. If I wasn't a man of science, I'd say it was some sort of miracle. I've never heard of anything like it. You're still weak, and will need careful attention for a few days, but you're out of danger.'

He turned to the others in the room. 'Plenty of rest. She'll need lots of clean water to keep her hydrated, and only plain food.'

'Plain food is all we've got,' Mrs F replied. 'There's a war on, you know.'

'Well, yes. Quite.' He ran his fingers along his moustache and did a strange little bow.

After that, he cleaned Nisha's cuts and put dressings on the worst of them. He shone a light in her eyes and asked her to follow his finger this way and that. He checked her ears too, and looked into her mouth. After he had given her the all-clear, Mrs F led him downstairs and showed him out. He was walking tall with a bounce in his step, and Nisha could tell that he was congratulating himself for a job well done.

'He's a strange little man,' Mrs Barrow muttered as she closed the bedroom door behind them. 'I never cared much for him.'

Nisha went to sit on Amma's bed.

'How long have I been like this?' Amma asked.

'Days,' Nisha said. 'It feels like such a long time.'

'You gave Nisha quite a scare,' Mrs Barrow said. 'You gave us *all* a scare.'

Amma looked up at her. 'Has there been any news from Charles? Did he get away from Singapore?'

Mrs Barrow lowered her eyes. 'Nothing yet, I'm afraid. We—'

'We're hoping,' Nisha said, looking at her grandmother. 'Aren't we? We have hope.'

'Yes.' Mrs Barrow smiled sadly. 'We have hope.'

'There's always room for that,' Amma agreed. 'Thank you for looking after Nisha.'

Mrs Barrow didn't try to hide her embarrassment. 'I'm afraid I might have been a bit of a dragon. I'm not used to having people in the house, you see – especially not children. I rather think she's looked after me.'

Amma looked puzzled.

'Your daughter is quite a spark,' Grandmother said. 'And she has the courage of a lion. She saved my life this evening.'

Amma turned to Nisha, who told her what had happened on the causeway. By the time she was finished, Amma's eyes were closed and she was breathing deeply.

'Let's leave her to sleep,' Mrs Barrow whispered.

Nisha was going to object. She didn't want to leave Amma even for a second, but her grandmother put a hand on her shoulder and smiled gently. 'I think that's enough adventure for one evening, don't you? I'll ask Mrs Foster to draw you a bath, and I'll fetch you a clean dress for tomorrow. Perhaps I can find one that doesn't itch around the collar.'

Outside, in the corridor, Nisha stopped and took her grandmother's hands.

'What is it?' Mrs Barrow asked.

Nisha looked up into her face. 'I've seen Twig.'

'I beg your pardon?' Mrs Barrow blinked in surprise.

'At first I thought Twig was a boy, but I was wrong.'

Mrs Barrow tried to step back but Nisha held her hands tight.

'Twig's a girl,' Nisha said. 'Or, rather, a girl who wants to be a boy.'

Mrs Barrow went pale.

'He's Elizabeth,' Nisha said. 'Twig is Elizabeth, isn't he?'

Mrs Barrow swallowed hard. Her mouth was dry when she spoke. Her voice was quiet. 'I thought I heard you say her name that day in my study. And again, in the churchyard, but I . . . I couldn't quite believe it. It brought back so many memories. All the little things I had forgotten about her. Twig is what your father called his sister. It was his nickname for her. He said she was skinny as a twig, and wanted to live in a tree like one. But you can't have seen her. She's—'

'I *have* seen her,' Nisha said.

'But . . .'

'She's on the island. In the Weeping Tree. In the wind.

Have you never heard her call your name?'

Mrs Barrow's eyes glazed over. 'I sometimes hear things,' she said. 'But it's just a trick of the wind.'

'No. It's Elizabeth. And there's something she wants me to tell you.'

Mrs Barrow waited with tears spilling down her cheeks.

'She wants you to know that it wasn't your fault,' Nisha said. 'She says she knows you blame yourself, but there was nothing you could have done to save her. It was never your fault.'

Mrs Barrow opened her mouth, but no words came out.

57

VIRTUS. SPES. HONESTAS.

Joy came to the island later that night. She brought colour and life and laughter, just like always.

Dry and warm, Nisha was exhausted but still awake. She was in the kitchen when Joy arrived, eating Woolton pie with vegetable gravy. She couldn't wait to tell Joy everything that had happened. Except for the part about Twig. That was just for her and her grandmother. No one else needed to know about that.

When Nisha had finished, Joy placed her teacup on its saucer and dusted off her hands. 'Then my job here is done. You don't need me any more.'

'Of course we need you here, you silly goose,' Nisha

protested. 'Who else will dance with me?'

'Who you callin' silly goose?' Joy pretended to be shocked.

'Nisha's mam still needs lookin' after,' Mrs F told her. 'I think we'll need you for a few nights yet. An' after that, you're welcome here any time you like. I'm sure Mrs Barrow won't mind, and there's nee chance I'm dancin' round the kitchen like a daft brush, so I'll need you for that.'

'That's settled then.' Nisha pretended to spit on her hand, and held it out for Joy to shake.

'Done.' Joy shook with her.

'Right,' said Mrs F, looking at Nisha. 'You've had your supper and you've seen Joy, so it's off to bed.'

'I'll take you up,' Joy said to Nisha. 'But there's something I want to show you first. Something to do with what you asked me the other day. I remembered it on the way here tonight. It's strange I didn't think of it before.' She stood up and held out her hand. 'Come with me.'

Nisha followed Joy upstairs and they crept into Amma's bedroom. Amma was fast asleep and breathing normally.

'Look,' Joy whispered. 'It's been staring us in the face every night and I've hardly even noticed it. You must have done the same thing. Strange, when you think about it.'

She went to the mantel over the fireplace and held up

the lamp she had brought with her. She pointed to the image carved into the stone. It was chipped and scuffed almost beyond recognition, but Nisha could just make out one word.

honestas.

'That's what you asked me about, isn't it?' Joy said. 'That's the word you—'

But Nisha wasn't paying attention any more. The image on this mantel was too faint and broken to see properly, but she was almost certain she knew where there was another one. A perfect one.

'I have to speak to my grandmother. It's late but I think she's still in her study.'

Consumed by curiosity and excitement, Nisha made her way downstairs as quickly as she could. She crossed the hallway to her grandmother's study and knocked on the door.

'Is everything all right?' Mrs Barrow asked when Nisha entered.

The fire was crackling and she was sitting in a comfortable armchair with a blanket over her knees and a book in her hands. On the table beside her was a lamp and a fresh cup of tea that was still steaming.

'I was wondering if . . .' Nisha tried to gather her words. 'I was wondering if I may look in Elizabeth's room. There's something I'd like to see.'

'What is it?'

'I'm not sure. Something on the mantelpiece.'

'I'm intrigued.' Mrs Barrow thought for a moment then lifted the book and blanket from her lap. 'And how can I refuse the girl who saved my life?' she said as she went to her desk and opened the top drawer. She took out a key and held it up for Nisha to see. 'After you, my dear.'

'Please don't move anything,' Mrs Barrow said when she opened the door at the top of the concealed staircase. 'Or touch anything.'

'I promise,' Nisha said. 'I just want to see something.'

The room was exactly as it had been when Nisha was last there. Only the daphnes in the vase were new. Their fragrance filled the room.

Nisha went straight to the mantel over the fireplace and asked her grandmother to hold up the lamp.

And there it was. A perfect version of the carving she had just been looking at in Amma's room.

'What is that?' Nisha asked.

'Well, that's our family crest,' Mrs Barrow said.

The crest was shaped like a shield with a wolf in the centre and two crossed axes above it. On either side of the axes was a tree.

Underneath the shield was a simple scroll with three words carved into it.

virtus. spes. honestas.

'Courage. Hope. Honesty,' Nisha whispered.

'That's right,' said Mrs Barrow. 'Our family motto. Elizabeth always said they were the words she wanted to live by. Your father, too. Courage, hope and honesty.'

And for now, Nisha thought, hope was the most important.

For Papa, she had to have hope.

Extract from Nisha Barrow's Truth, 1942

Grandmother has been teaching me the names of the flowers. There are bright yellow daffodils, and peonies that are the same colour as the sun setting over the jungle. The azaleas are like little fires in the far corner of the garden, and there are pansies and primroses and bluebells and others that I don't know the names of yet. Everything feels so alive and colourful now, as if the island has come to life. Or as if I have. There's red ivy on the walls of Barrow House, and the long grass is the colour of tree snakes. The gorse bushes are so yellow they make my eyes hurt! Even the Weeping Tree is covered with new leaves, and the first blossoms are showing. Grandmother keeps saying it hasn't blossomed like that for years. And even then, she has never seen it look so beautiful. When the sun shines there's nowhere lovelier than Barrow Island (apart from home, of course). And when I went to the village yesterday, I noticed something really strange. The houses aren't built from grey stone like I thought. It's more like a sandy colour, and it's actually quite lovely.

Amma sits with me in the garden some afternoons. She's still weak, but improving every day. Other times I sit alone with my journal and my little red stone (like right now) and I close my eyes and feel the wind on my face and wonder if Twig was even real. Was everything just a dream? I sometimes think it must have been a dream otherwise it doesn't make sense.

I don't have anything to show for what happened. The bracelet is gone as if it never existed. I haven't seen Twig since the night of Hitler's bomb – but I do sometimes hear his voice in the wind, whispering my name.

Grandmother seems happier, as if that heavy weight has lifted from her shoulders. It hasn't gone completely, she's still stern and strict, and a bit of a dragon sometimes, but she's softer now. She smiles more often and spends less time locked away in her study. I think Humphrey is pleased about that.

Jamie is still Jamie. He's as cheeky and brilliant as ever. He comes every day to help Mr Foster. He's amazing with Bonny (that pony loves Jamie more than anything!) and he's useful in the garden. He always goes home with a dirty face and mud under his fingernails ('clarty' as Jamie always says!). He gets his lunch and a shilling a week for his efforts and I think Mr Foster is secretly happy to have his company. Sometimes Jamie slips away from his duties, and we go down to the beach to look for shells. Mr Foster pretends not to notice.

Joy comes from time to time. Yesterday she got a letter to say she's going to Newcastle to learn how to be a nurse soon. I will miss her but she has promised to keep coming back. She's so much fun and I want to be exactly like her when I get older. She brings laughter and music with her as if it's her perfume, and we sit in the kitchen, listening to the wireless. When a good tune comes on, we dance around the table while Jamie plays the spoons, and Mr Foster drums his fingers on a tin. Mrs F rolls her eyes (of course!), but I know she's happy to see life and colour in her kitchen.

There's still no word from Papa, but I have hope, and I know he will come home. I know it.

I'll always have hope, because that's what Twig taught me. So every day I walk along the overgrown path to the Weeping Tree to remember that, and to tell him about Papa – his twin brother.

I tell him something else, too. I tell him he isn't the heart of the Weeping Tree. He's the heart of Barrow House.

The Heart of Barrow Island.

Name of Ship _Empire Hope_

Steamship Line _____ GLASGOW AND COMMONWEALTH

NAMES AND DESCRIPTIONS OF BRITISH PASS

(1)	(2)	(3)	(4)
Contract Ticket Number	NAMES OF PASSENGERS	Last address in the United Kingdom	CLASS (Whether 1st, 2nd or 3rd)
	Turner Mr John	4 Compton Dr. Bradford	
	Marshall Mr Peter	Garnet St Oldham	
	Hinton Mrs James		
	Smith Miss Nancy	Park Road North Chester-le-st	
	Toole Mr Reginald		
	Cheetham Mr Jack	Linden Rd. Newcastle	
	Andersen Mr Howard		
	Knudsen Mr Jorgen		
	Barrow Mr Charles	Barrow Island. Morbury. Northumberlan	
	Saunders Mrs Arthur		
	Matthews Mr Henry	Clayton St. Bishopthorpe	
	Seiffert Mr Dennis		
	Newman Mr Bernard	The Avenue Durham	
	Hill Mrs William		
	Griffin Mr Stephen		
	Finney Mr Martin		

Date of Departure _5th February_ **19** 42

Where Bound _ENGLAND_

...GERS EMBARKED AT THE PORT OF _Singapore_

(5) Port at which passengers have contracted to land.	(6) Profession, Occupation or Calling of Passengers	(7) AGES OF PASSENGERS								(8) Country of Last Permanent Residence						(9) Country of Intended Future Permanent Residency
		Adults of 12 years and upwards				Children between 1 & 11		Infants		England.	Wales.	Scotland.	Northern Ireland.	Other Parts of the British Empire.	Foreign Countries.	
		Accompanied by husband or wife		Not accompanied by husband or wife												
		Males.	Females.	Males.	Females.	Males.	Females.	Males.	Females.							
acuation				1											1	England
				1											1	
				1											1	
					1										1	
				1											1	
				1											1	
				1											1	
				1											1	
				1											1	
					1										1	
				1											1	
				1											1	
															1	
					1										1	
				1											1	
				1											1	

DID YOU KNOW?

The Japanese invasion of Malaya on 8th December 1941 happened at almost exactly the same time as the more well-known Japanese attack on Pearl Harbor.

The attack began on the north-east coast of Malaya, at a place called Kota Bharu. British, Indian and Australian soldiers fought hard to stop the Japanese from landing on the beaches, but they were overwhelmed and had to retreat.

The Japanese did not take prisoners. This helped them move swiftly through Malaya. They also moved quickly through the rubber plantations and the jungle by using bicycles.

Allied forces greatly underestimated the strength and skill of the Japanese. Allies believed the Japanese soldiers and planes would be inferior to their own, but they were wrong.

On 11th January 1942, just three days after the first attack, Japanese forces took Kuala Lumpur, the capital city of Malaya. British-led forces retreated and destroyed the causeway that joined Malaya and Singapore.

On 8th February 1942, Japanese troops entered Singapore.

After a week of fighting, British-led forces surrendered Singapore to the Japanese. Winston Churchill called it the 'worst disaster' in British military history.

Due to unrealistically positive statements by the British authorities, many civilians and their families delayed their evacuation. However, when it became clear that the Japanese were unstoppable, civilians flooded towards Singapore in the hope of escape.

The last evacuation ships left Singapore just a few days before the surrender. Japanese planes continued to bombard the docks throughout the evacuation. In those final days, most of the evacuation ships were destroyed. Hundreds of civilians were killed. Many of those left behind were captured by the Japanese and sent to prison camps.

But some ships escaped . . .

GLOSSARY

Northumbrian Dialect

botha – bother/trouble

bray – to hit, thump or beat

canny – good/very

clarty – dirty

dee – do

deein' – doing

divvent – do not

fatha – father

fettle – mood/health

gan – go

gannin' – going

geet – very

heed – head

howay – come on

hoy – throw/put

knaa – know

lekky – electricity

nee – no

nowt – nothing

plodgin' – wading in water, especially the sea

reet – right

summat – something

telt – told

wisht – hush

Words in Malay

hantu – ghost

jambu – a small, round or bell-shaped fragrant fruit native to Malaysia

kedai – shop

Kota Bharu – a city on the east coast of Malaysia

mahjong – a tile-based game developed in China

Malaya – the part of Malaysia now known as Peninsular Malaysia or Western Malaysia

nasi bungkus – steamed rice mixed with meat, vegetables and chilli sauce, wrapped in a banana leaf

pokok – tree

rambutan – a tropical fruit with leathery skin that appears to be hairy ('rambutan' literally means 'hairy'), with a sweet whitish flesh similar to a lychee inside

songkok – a traditional hat, usually made of black felt

Other Words and Phrases

carbolic soap – a mildly antiseptic soap

Gladstone bag – a deep bag made of stiff leather, often used by doctors to carry medical equipment

Ironside's Crust – concrete cubes placed around the British coast to delay a possible German landing

Kitchen Front – a popular wartime food programme broadcast on the wireless

National Flour – a basic nutritious flour, grey in colour, used during WWII instead of white flour

National Loaf – bread made using National Flour
wireless – a wireless radio
Woolton pie – an unpopular vegetable pie, created
because meat was in short supply during WWII

ACKNOWLEDGEMENTS

Don't worry, I'll keep this short. I just want to say thank you to everyone at Chicken House for believing in Nisha and the strange things that happen on Barrow Island. Their help and advice have been invaluable in bringing Nisha's story to life. Thanks also to my agent, Ella, who always has my back, and to Alex Smith from Northcote Lodge, who helped with the Latin words I have used. Especially, though, thanks to my children for the joy they bring me every day, and to my wife who gives me courage and hope in all things.

virtus. spes. honestas.